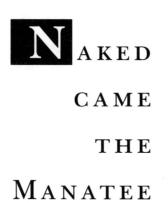AKED

CAME

THE

MANATEE

Naked Came the Manatee

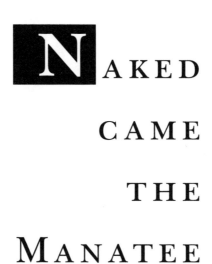

a

novel

by

Carl Hiaasen

Dave Barry

Elmore Leonard

Edna Buchanan

James W. Hall

Les Standiford

Paul Levine

Brian Antoni

Tananarive Due

John Dufresne

Vicki Hendricks

Carolina Hospital

Evelyn Mayerson

G. P. Putnam's Sons
New York

G. P. Putnam's Sons
Publishers Since 1838
200 Madison Avenue
New York, NY 10016

Library of Congress Cataloging-in-Publication Data

Naked came the manatee : a novel / by Carl Hiaasen . . . [et al.].
    p.   cm.
  ISBN 0-399-14192-8
  1. Florida—Fiction.   I. Hiaasen, Carl.
PS3550.A1N36   1996   96-15707 CIP
813'.54—dc20

Printed in the United States of America
10 9 8 7 6 5 4 3 2 1

This book is printed on acid-free paper. ∞

Book design by Songhee Kim

CONTENTS

BOOGER

Dave Barry

ATURDAY NIGHT,
Coconut Grove.

It was the usual scene: thousands of people, not one of whom a normal person would call normal.

There were the European tourists, getting off their big fume-belching buses, wearing their new jeans and their Hard Rock Cafe T-shirts, which they bought when their charter bus stopped in Orlando. They moved in chattering clots, following their flag-waving tour directors, lining up outside Planet Hollywood, checking out the wall where famous movie stars had made impressions of their hands in the cement squares, taking videos of each other putting their palms in the *exact same spot* where Bruce Willis once put his palm.

Eventually they'd be admitted, past the velvet ropes, get an actual table, order an *actual cheeseburger.* This, truly, was America: eating cheeseburgers with other European tourists.

Outside, the pulsating mutant throng was gearing up for the all-night street party, fashion bazaar, and freak show that the Grove becomes on weekend nights. Squadrons of young singles—bodies taut, hair perfect, clothes fashionable, minds empty—relentlessly roamed the CocoWalk Multi-Level Shopping and Pickup Complex, checking each other out, admiring themselves. Everywhere for blocks around, there were peddlers peddling, posers posing, gawkers gawking, drunks drinking, bums bumming, and hustlers hustling. Traffic had already congealed into a dense, noisy, confused mass of cruising tourist-bearing rickshaws, blatting Harleys, megawatt-booming cruise cars, and the pathetic, plaintively honking fools who actually thought they could drive *through* the Grove on a Saturday night. It was just getting started. It would go on until dawn, and beyond.

Sitting on the porch of her snug, hurricane-weathered cottage nestled beneath a pair of massive ficus trees not three hundred yards away, Marion McAlister Williams listened to the distant din wafting toward her on the South Florida night. She could still hear pretty well, and she could think as well as anybody—better than most, in fact. Not bad, when you considered that she was 102 years old, had come to Miami on a sailboat when Coconut Grove was a two-family, no-road hamlet, and Seminoles fished the bay.

Not much fish to catch in there now, she thought bitterly, not much life at all in that poor overused, over-dredged public sewer. Oh, she'd done what she could. She'd written that book, back in the forties, way ahead of her time; she'd told the world what the movers and shakers of South Florida were doing to the bay. The book got a lot of attention, won her a couple of big awards. After a while even the movers and shakers noticed, started inviting her to dinners, giving her plaques, calling her a South Florida Treasure, like she was some kind of endangered turtle. Then they'd pat her on her frail, stooped shoulders, send her off home, and go right back to screwing up the bay.

From her porch, she could smell the water, close by to the southeast. She wondered, as she often did, what was going on out there, away from the lunacy of the Grove, in the dark.

■　　■　　■

A mile or so down the coast, where rich people live in huge, expensive, fashionable, professionally decorated, truly uncomfortable homes, Booger flippered his massive blob of a body slowly through the murky water just off-shore. Of course, he didn't know he was called Booger by the boat-dwellers in the Grove, where he spent most of his time. Being a manatee, he wasn't big on abstract concepts such as names. He also hadn't figured out, despite several collisions and one painful propeller-inflicted wound, that he should try to avoid motorboats.

And thus, although he could sense it coming, he made no effort whatsoever to avoid the beat-up old outboard-powered skiff racing directly toward him in the dark. And since the two men in the skiff were (a) running without lights and (b) arguing, they did not notice Booger's bulk dead ahead, almost all of it just below the surface, just like the iceberg that caused all that trouble for the *Titanic*.

■　■　■

"This ain't no damn computer, I can tell you that for damn sure," Hector was saying, from the front of the skiff. He was frowning at the wooden crate sitting on a seat cushion and strapped to the seat with a pair of bungee cords. He kicked aside the scummy towrope at his feet and leaned down to poke around in the straw between the slats of the crate for a clearer glimpse at the plastic-wrapped, roundish object, hard and smooth like some kind of metal, pressing up against the wood.

"How the hell do you know?" asked Phil, from the stern, where he had his hand on the outboard tiller.

"Because it ain't even got a power plug," said Hector. "Computers got power plugs."

"What the hell do you care what it is?" said Phil. "We take it to the rich man's dock, we give it to the rich man, he gives us the other five thou, we're gone. Ten thou, total, five each, minus my boat expenses, easy money. You got a better plan? You maybe wanna rob another UPS truck?''

This was a reference to Hector's last major moneymaking idea, which was to snatch a box at random from the back of a UPS van parked on Kendall Drive. Unfortunately, Hector, who was also the getaway-car driver, had tried to get away a little too fast; he'd driven directly into a Lexus making a left turn across traffic, causing it to smash into a Jaguar. As it happened—this was, after all, South Florida—both the Lexus *and* the Jaguar were being driven by well-known, highly successful, politically connected narcotics traffickers, so Hector and Phil had gotten into *big* trouble with the law. They'd wound up doing eighteen months in jail.

The box they had stolen from the UPS truck—Phil would never let Hector forget this—turned out to contain dirty undershorts that a University of Miami prelaw student was sending home to his mom for laundering.

"Very funny," said Hector. "Ha ha. But you tell me, why'd the Cuban tell us it's a computer if it ain't? And that wasn't no local Cuban neither. That was a *Cuban* Cuban, from Cuba. That was a Cuban navy boat following his boat. It was running with no lights, trying to stay outta sight, but I saw it.''

"Hector, you told me that fifty-three times, and I still don't care. I don't care if he was from *Mars,* OK? Ten thou is ten thou.''

"I think it's nuclear," said Hector quietly. He pronounced it "nuke-u-lar," like Walter Cronkite.

"It's *what?*" asked Phil.

"Nuclear. Like a bomb. The way the Cuban handled it, you know? The way he was, so, like, *scared* of it. And did you see him open that little door in it, just before he put it in the crate? There was some kind of *numbers* in there, man."

"Computers got numbers," noted Phil.

"These ain't computer numbers," said Hector. "These are little lights, like *glowing* numbers."

"Only number I care about," said Phil, "is ten thousand dollars. You can buy a lot of underwear for that."

Hector said a very bad thing to Phil.

∎ ∎ ∎

Back in the heart of the Grove, city of Miami rookie police officer Joe Sereno was trying to explain to an extremely large, extremely drunk male tourist that, no matter what the system was back in his hometown, the system here in Miami was, if you had to urinate, you did it in some kind of enclosed toilet facility. You did not do it out in public. You especially did not do it off the second-floor balcony of the CocoWalk complex.

"Sir," Sereno was saying, "why don't you—"

"I got the right to remain silent!" the tourist announced. He virtually never missed *The People's Court*.

"Sir," said Sereno, "I'm not arresting you. I'm just asking you to zip up your—"

"ANYTHING I SAY *CAN* AND *WILL* be USED AGAINST ME!" bellowed the large man. The fast-growing crowd of onlookers cheered. Many were aiming video cameras. This was excellent entertainment, even better than the Hare Krishnas.

Joe Sereno sighed. This was *not* what he had in mind when he joined the police department. He wanted to make a difference, to do something useful, to *fight crime,* for God's sake, not to spend his nights chaperoning the block party from hell, baby-sitting a bunch of *morons* who—

"I HAVE THE RIGHT TO AN ATTORNEY!!!" the large man screamed. "SOMEBODY GET ME . . . what's his name."

"Perry Mason?" suggested a voice from the crowd.

"NO, DAMMIT! THE OTHER ONE!"

"Johnnie Cochran?"

"YES! HIM! SOMEBODY GET ME JOHNNIE COCH . . . COCH . . . *Cocchhuurrrrgggghhh . . .*"

Although he was a rookie, Sereno had worked the Grove long enough to see what was coming, and thus stepped back quickly enough to avoid the sudden eruption. Not everyone on the sidewalk below was so lucky. Bedlam erupted as the crowd, screaming, surged away from the area directly underneath the puking giant. A rickshaw, coming around the corner, was knocked over by the fleeing mob, sending an older couple sprawling into the street, directly into the path of a Harley-Davidson, whose driver turned right sharply in an effort to avoid them, hit the curb, and was launched across the sidewalk into the fountain.

Sereno sprinted for the stairs, glancing at his watch. Nine o'clock, straight up.

The night was young.

■　　■　　■

Another boring night, Fay Leonard thought, as she locked up her dive shop on South Dixie Highway. She was beginning to wonder about the shop. It had seemed like such a good idea—a chance for her to make a living doing the one thing she truly loved. Problem was, she wasn't doing any diving; she was always running the shop. It ate up her days, and it was starting to eat up her nights. Like, tonight, she had to take two full sets of rental scuba gear over to a charter boat at Dinner Key Marina, which meant driving into the Grove, which was of course going to be a zoo on a Saturday night.

Lugging the heavy air tanks out to her pickup truck, she thought, All this work, carrying all this gear around, and I don't even get to use it.

■　　■　　■

Still sitting on her porch, Marion McAlister Williams sat upright, coming abruptly out of her doze. She glanced around; nothing amiss.

And yet something was wrong. She knew it. Something out in the bay. She knew that bay, knew it better than anybody else, knew things about it she could never explain. And right then, right that second, she knew something was going wrong. Bad wrong.

She clutched her chair and listened to the night, listened hard, but all she heard was the Grove din, and frogs.

But there was something. She *knew* it.

∎　∎　∎

Just an inch or two below the bay surface, Booger felt the pressure wave of the approaching skiff. He'd had that feeling before, and he felt vaguely uncomfortable about it, but even if he'd known enough to get out of the way, there wasn't really any time.

∎　∎　∎

"Tell you one thing," Phil was saying. "If I *did* steal somebody's underwear, you can bet it would at least be *clean* underwear."

That did it. Hector, enraged, rose in the front of the skiff, turned toward Phil, pointed, and shouted, "YOU KNOW WHAT YOU CAN DO, PHIL? YOU WANT TO KNOW WHAT YOU CAN DO? YOU CAN—"

But Hector never did get to tell Phil what he could do, because at precisely that moment the skiff rammed into Booger and came to an extremely sudden stop. Hector, however, kept right on going, right off the bow, still pointing vaguely in the direction of Phil, who sprawled, face first, to the floor of the skiff.

The force of the collision likewise hurled Phil's and Hector's mystery cargo forward, splintering the flimsy fiberglass where the bungee cords were attached to the seat. It slammed against the bow with a crunching sound, then launched into the air in an explosion of bilge water and towrope; then the whole mass splashed into the bay about thirty feet in front of the skiff, the seat cushion floating upside down and the crushed crate dangling a few feet below from the bungee cords, trailing yards of towrope.

Into this mess swam a very alarmed Booger, moving away from the skiff as fast as a manatee can move. His snout passed directly under the floating cushion, so that as he surged forward, the bungee cords secured the flotsam firmly to his massive body. Booger continued to flipper frantically forward in the gloom, saddled with the awkward weight of trash.

Booger barely noticed it. His brain—such as it was—was focused entirely on one idea: *getting out of there,* to someplace safe. And being a creature of habit, he knew exactly where he was going.

Like so many others on this particular night, Booger was headed for Coconut Grove.

2

THE BIG
WET SLEEP

Les Standiford

GRAND AVENUE, TEN p.m., a Saturday night. John Deal sat in his car opposite a tiny neighborhood market, a mile or more from his destination on the far side of Coconut Grove. He was locked in a dead stall, part of an endless line of unmoving traffic, gripping and ungripping the wheel of the vehicle he had come to refer to as the "Hog."

The Hog had begun its automotive life as a Cadillac Seville—but it had long since been transformed into a kind of gentleman's El Camino, the passenger cabin cut in half, a tiny pickup bed created where the back seat and trunk had been. Not the sort of thing the folks at Cadillac would approve of, but it wasn't Deal's fault. He'd had to take it in payment on a construction project gone bad; now he couldn't afford anything else.

The fact that he was stuck in gridlock was his fault, however. Trying to make his way through the Grove on a Saturday night—what had he been thinking of? He should have gone farther north on U.S. 1, made his way back down to Janice's apartment through the twisty little streets that the Saturday Night Drive crowd hadn't discovered yet. But he'd been distracted, rehearsing his speech, reminding himself to stay composed no matter what Janice said or did . . . and now look what he'd done to himself.

He glanced in the mirror at a chopped and channeled Accord that had nosed up to within inches of his rear bumper: there seemed little chance of backing up, making a U-ey out of this line. Worse, a relentless kind of music was blaring from the Accord, its pulsing bass line so powerful that Deal's mirror vibrated, sending the black Accord into a shimmering mirage image, settling back into sharp definition, then blurring again. Horns ahead and behind joined the chorus.

Deal noticed an old black man sitting on a backless kitchen chair outside the market, a cigarette burning between his fingers. His doleful gaze locked with Deal's for a moment, then turned away. Deal felt as if he'd been marked, somehow:

Another Yuppie lemming, a guy so rich he could afford to fart around with a perfectly good Cadillac car, on his way through shantytown, headed for the mindless glitz up ahead.

He could get out, Deal thought, leave the Hog where it

was, take a seat beside the old guy, try to convince him otherwise. Explain how he was on his way to see his estranged wife, convince her to come back home again, how he was having trouble with his finances, how we were all in this mess together, just like the Benetton ads said. The old guy could give him his blessing, they could wear colorful sweaters together and be friends.

Sure. And pigs could sing the Hallelujah Chorus.

He did get out of the Hog, though, leaving the door wide open as he stepped up into the Hog's bed for a better look at what might be happening. Slow was one thing, but they hadn't moved at all, not for a good ten minutes.

What he saw filled him with dismay. The junction of Main and Grand, a kind of mini–Times Square just opposite the multileveled CocoWalk mall, was bad enough on a normal Saturday—endless streams of pedestrians ignoring the signals, la-de-dah-ing through the inching traffic, stopping to chat with the drivers, dodging rickshaw drivers and bikers weaving through it all. But this was way beyond normal.

A pulsing, unmoving throng had jammed the intersection. A roar wafted down the line toward him, and he caught a glimpse of a huge, naked man being borne aloft on the uplifted arms of the crowd. Then he saw another figure bouncing atop the crowd—a policeman, he realized. Beer foam shot in streamers from cheering onlookers massed at the CocoWalk railings. Cans arced down, bottles, what looked like a shoe. Then shirts, other articles of clothing fluttering in the breeze.

Another roar from the crowd as a topless girl jumped

onto the hood of a car and began an energetic boogie. Deal stepped down from the bed of the Hog, got back in the driver's seat. The mob would make its way right down the line of stalled traffic, he thought. How many of them would it take to lift the Hog, tip it over, turn it into a trampoline?

Deal felt a jolt, then realized the Accord behind him had popped his bumper. He glanced in the mirror. The driver of the Accord, a kid with a ball cap turned backward, was leaning halfway out his window, talking to someone in a car headed in the opposite direction. The Accord bumped him again, hard enough to rock Deal in his seat. The kid was still talking, oblivious.

Deal glanced ahead. There was a bona fide pickup truck in front of him, with what looked like a pile of scuba gear in the back. The crowd was going to love that, he thought—dive naked, dive free. He also noted that the pickup had moved slightly, allowing him a couple feet of clearance. Deal checked the mirror again, dropped the Hog in reverse.

He eased back until he felt his bumper engage the Accord's, then gave the Hog some pedal. He felt resistance, pressed down harder. The Hog's engine growled, all eight cylinders getting seriously involved. He heard a cry—maybe his tires', maybe the kid's—saw through the mirror that smoke was rising from the Hog's rear tires, saw that the kid had lost his balance, was tumbling out his window as the Accord lurched backward.

When he figured he had made enough room, Deal let off the gas, dropped the Hog into drive, leaned hard on the wheel. The Hog turned neatly on its redone suspension, swung about, darted into a gap that had formed as the line of traffic heading out of the Grove began to move. Deal stopped, rolled down his window, motioned to the startled driver of the pickup with the scuba gear. A remarkably attractive woman, he noted. Like him, she seemed old enough to have known better.

"Turn around," he called, motioning to the space that had opened in front of the Hog. She hesitated, staring uncertainly at him. This was Miami, after all. He ignored the wild chorus of horns behind him. "It's a riot," he said. "You don't want to go that way."

She craned her neck for a look just as the pop-pop-pop of gunfire erupted from somewhere. That did it. She threw the truck in reverse, chewed rubber all along the space where the Hog had been. She stopped just short of the still-driverless Accord, dropped into low, and swung the pickup around in front of Deal. In the next instant she was speeding away toward U.S. 1, the scuba gear dancing, a hand and slender arm waving a thank-you as she disappeared. Something about the little drama left Deal with a curious pang, but the horns were deafening at his back and he didn't have long to consider it.

He floored the Hog, roared past the stalled traffic himself. The kid who had been driving the Accord was just struggling up off his hands and knees. You think that was something, wait till you see what's coming next, Deal thought, then had to yank the Hog into an abrupt turn to avoid a new bottleneck headed out of the Grove.

He found himself traveling down an unfamiliar narrow lane now, a tunnel boring through a dense overhang of ficus, Florida holly, and strangler fig. He was forced into another turn and another—like running a maze—and was still trying to brush aside the image of the striking woman behind the wheel of the dive truck. Was it someone he'd met? he wondered. Or someone he wished he had? In the next instant, he was clutching the wheel tightly as the Hog bottomed out in a huge, rain-filled pothole, spraying water like a Donzi off its prow.

The filthy water was just clearing from his windshield when Deal saw the man, or what he presumed was a man. Though the whole thing couldn't have taken more than a few seconds, Deal's mind registered details with the precision and clarity that only impending disaster can bring. The figure stood in the middle of the gloomy tunnel of foliage, arm upflung in surprise, face twisted in the glare of the Hog's headlights. He seemed to be draped in a tangle of old shrimp netting which itself was studded with still-dripping seaweed, battered lobster-trap buoys, and the assorted detritus you'd expect to find floating the backwaters of the nearby bay these days. There was something odd about the guy's face, a lopsided quality that suggested he'd already had one accident in the not so distant past. He held a broken oar in his other hand— something he might have been using as a cane, or a makeshift crutch, and which had probably saved his life.

The man—the ancient mariner, Deal found himself thinking—vaulted backward, using the point of the oar for leverage, just as Deal slammed on the brakes. The Hog seemed to sail on imperturbably for a moment, until the water sloughed off the linings of the brakes. When they did catch hold, it was with a vengeance. He felt the heavy rear of the car rip loose from the pavement and whip around violently, a force like a giant hand pressing him back in the seat. He was sure that next he'd feel the muffled thud of mariner body meeting sheet metal, but the moment passed, and instead he caught a glimpse of the man's astonished face peering at him as the Hog shot past.

The pale, distorted face receded as if Deal were the stationary one; he watched helplessly as the man was yanked into oblivion by some otherworldly force. Then the front end of the Hog tipped up abruptly, and Deal felt himself plunging down into his own abyss. There was a crunching sound, metal against rock, another, and another, a jolt as his head rammed the roof, a second as it bashed against the wheel.

He was seeing only bright flashes of light now, had lost all sense of orientation. Upside down, sideways, going forward, or back? Impossible to know. He heard a tremendous splash, felt another jolt and a momentary weightlessness before gravity finally caught up with him. Gentle rocking now, and then a slow but steady descent. The smell of seawater, brackish rot, odor of the grave, he thought.

He was in the water and going down. Groggy, he felt his hands grope blindly, frantically for the handle of the door. He sensed a great coolness envelop his chest, his groin, his neck. Strange objects bumped at his face, slid away, curled back again. He felt the door lever slide into his grasp like some odd creature from the deep. He pulled. Kicked reflexively at the door, felt resistance, unlatched his seat belt in a kind of daze.

He felt release then, free drifting in water that was cool

and somehow warm at once. His limbs were heavy now, his head lolling in the current. Whatever instinctual source of energy had enabled him to escape had expended itself. He floated beneath the surface, his consciousness teetering, sensing that soon he would open his mouth and take that great last gasp that would fill his lungs with water and sink him like a stone. Worst of all, there was nothing he could do about it, not one thing.

He felt the pressure building in his chest, accompanied by a mounting fire in his brain. He willed his arms to move, his legs to kick, but the signals flew off down blind trails, leaving him adrift, rudderless, a ship with a captain shouting orders from the bridge and no one left in the engine room. As he drifted into darkness, he dreamed that something—a hand, or perhaps a diver's fin—came to brush against his chest, and then he became aware of a great presence swelling up beneath him. In this dream or vision, he began to rise through the murky water, picking up speed, spiraling upward toward some brilliant pool of light. Aside from the rather hackneyed image of the light, it seemed a lovely dream to him, one in which he felt his face break the surface of the water as if it were a tangible membrane, a passage into some other world, where he could gulp down air like any other man, and simply live and be.

■　■　■

"Just lie still, you." The woman's voice came to him from the darkness. A small voice, ancient, and yet carrying the authority of its years. He blinked his eyes, realized that it wasn't just darkness, that in fact he couldn't see. He raised his hands in a panic, felt hers pull him down.

"You've got some nasty bumps and cuts there," she said. "I've got a poultice resting. It's not to be disturbed." Deal felt the pressure of cloth, at his face. Yes, maybe he could detect a nimbus of light. He blinked again, felt his lids rustle at the bandages, smelled vague medicinal odors.

"Hospital," he heard himself mumble.

She laughed. "There won't be any hospital tonight, unh-uh. They got the whole of Coconut Grove cordoned off, they do. Waitin' for the fuss to burn itself out."

Deal heard distant shouts, chanting, the double boom of a shotgun. He felt a wave of dizziness sweep over him. He lay back, remembering, trying to comprehend all that had happened.

"Where am I?" he managed, at last. He groped about him, felt crisp sheets, a blanket, realized his clothes were gone, that he was wearing some kind of flannel gown. A lady's nightgown? It couldn't be. Surely it couldn't.

"Keep your hands off those bandages, now, or I'll tie 'em down, you hear me." Deal nodded, rested his hands on his chest.

"You're one lucky boy," she cackled. "Lucky old Booger took a liking to you, lucky I was there to pull you out."

"Booger?"

"He's a manatee," she said. "He's the last sane creature that lives in these parts, and that includes me. All the fuss erupted downtown, I went over to have a chat with Booger, see if maybe he thought this was a sign."

"A sign?" Deal's head was swimming again.

"The beginning of the end," she said. "Booger and me got a running bet. Hundred and two, I think I'll be around to witness it, he says we got a ways to go yet. I found him in his little grotto, keeping you propped up on a chunk of boat seat."

The dream was coming back to him now. The vague presence, being propelled upward, toward a pool of light he'd taken for *the* light. He shook his head.

"Did you have a flashlight with you?" he asked.

"You think I can see in the dark?" she snorted. "Here, raise up some. I want you to take a drink of this."

He felt a wiry hand under his neck, sensed something warm and steaming at his lips. The smell was bitter, even searing. "What is it?" he said.

"Swamp yarbs," she said. "Now drink it, or I'll hold your nose and pour it down you."

Deal sensed it wasn't a bluff. He was so weak he had no doubt she was capable of doing exactly what she said. He nodded, helped her guide the cup to his lips.

Despite its wretched smell, the brew tasted amazingly good. Licorice, he thought. And something earthy. With an unidentifiable blend of herbs. It was bracing. And just as quickly, soporific. He was drifting again by the time his head hit the pillow.

"Booger showed me what you floated in on," she said.

"I don't know what you mean," Deal said.

"What you had tied to that boat seat," she said.

Deal shook his head. "I . . . I fell into the water," he said.

"Course you did," she said. "You wrecked your boat and damn near drowned."

"No," he said. He felt himself spiraling. "I didn't."

"Carrying a thing like that, I'd hate to admit it myself," she said.

Deal wanted to protest again, but he was just too tired.

"I showed it to Booger, though," she cackled. "Fried his apples, I'll tell you. See there, I told 'im. Here comes the end of the world, Booger, just like I said."

He hadn't the slightest idea what she was talking about, but she'd get no argument from him. Not this night. She was still cackling when he went under for good.

3

BISCAYNE BLUES

Paul Levine

UST HOW MUCH IS A whiplash worth?'' John Deal asked, twisting awkwardly in his cervical collar.

"That depends on whether Dr. Scheinblum is sober when he testifies," his lawyer, Jake Lassiter, answered.

Deal hadn't been in court since an action film star had sued him over a broken pump motor in a custom-built Jacuzzi. Lassiter had won the case, cleverly arguing that the tub hadn't been intended for a dozen persons, eleven of whom happened to be strippers from Club Plutonium, bobbing for apples and whatnot in the foamy water.

Deal had nearly been late this morning. Though a native of Miami who had built houses in virtually every neighborhood, he had become lost on a stretch of Eighth Street—Calle Ocho—recently renamed Olga Guillot Way. A few blocks to the west, the same street was called Celia Cruz Way, then Loring P. Evans Memorial Boulevard. He'd turned north on what had been a familiar avenue, now renamed General Maximo Gomez Boulevard, and followed a Porsche with the personalized plate LAWYER. Like boasting about having the clap, Deal thought.

Heading downtown, he'd vaguely wondered how he could get the street sign contract for the city, something he figured would keep him as busy as a coffin maker in a spaghetti western. The construction business was slow, and Deal was hoping for a decent settlement on his personal-injury claim, at least enough to lift the subcontractors' liens on his latest job and get his backhoe out of hock.

Once on Flagler Street, Deal had paid a shoeless guy five bucks to clean the windshield and watch over the rental Taurus in a rubble-strewn spot under the I-95 ramp. Walking two blocks to the courthouse, he'd woven through a crowd of demonstrators who were protesting conditions on a Caribbean island that Deal could not place on a map. On the courthouse steps, the Voodoo Squad, two janitors with buckets and brooms, were gathering up a dead chicken, a goat's head, and a cake with frosted icing, all intended to cast various spells on judges and juries. Overhead, the turkey vultures circled in the updrafts, while inside, their double-breasted, dark-suited cousins hustled clients at the elevators.

Now, as the day wound down, Deal sat in a fourth-floor

courtroom, listening as his lawyer wrapped up his opening statement. He hoped this was a good idea. He'd let
Jake talk him into it only because his debts were piling up
so high, but now, listening to Jake's best over-the-top,
never-overestimate-the-intelligence-of-the-jury histrionics,
he was having his doubts. Well, too late now. He didn't
know what strings Jake had pulled to get the case to court
so fast, but here they were.

"An unprotected hazard!" Jake Lassiter thundered,
moving closer to the jury box where he planted his 225
pounds like an oak among saplings. "A death trap! A
terrifying plunge into darkness and fear!" Lassiter paused
and studied the jury. By Miami standards, it was a typical
collection of strangers: a tattooed lobster pot poacher, a
nipple ring designer with a shaved head, a *santero* who
chanted prayers to Babalu Aye during recess, a cross-
dressing doorman from a South Beach club, and two
Kendall housewives who nervously clutched their purses.
"Thank heavens for John Deal's extraordinary physical
condition," Lassiter proclaimed reverently, "and thank
heavens for his fervent will to live."

Not to mention a manatee named Booger, Deal
thought. He hadn't told Lassiter he'd been saved from
drowning by a barnacle-encrusted sea mammal, then
nursed back to health by a 102-year-old woman who
brewed medicinal potions from swamp grass. And of
course, he hadn't mentioned the box.

The box.

The best he could figure, it must have been attached by
the bungee lines to the manatee named Booger. Some-

how Deal had gotten tangled in the bungee when he'd floated out of the Hog into the cold, wet darkness. It had all been too weird.

"The city of Miami recklessly maintained a hazard at its marina," Lassiter told the jury. "The city breached its duty of reasonable care in failing to properly light the street and failing to warn of the sheer drop-off to a watery grave."

"Objection, Your Honor!" shouted Russell B. Whittaker III. The city's insurance lawyer jumped to his feet and tugged at his suspenders. "That's closing argument, not opening statement."

"Sustained," Judge Manuel Dominguez announced gravely, then shot a look at the wall clock. He hated to miss the first game at Miami Jai-alai. "Move it along, Mr. Lassiter." Maria, the court clerk and the judge's favorite niece, held up eight fingers, alerting Lassiter to his remaining time. The judge's secretary, Ileana Josefina Dominguez-Zaldivar, slipped into the courtroom from chambers and whispered something into the judge's ear, though she probably didn't call him "Your Honor." Ileana was his older sister, and insisted on calling the judge Manuelito, even in court. Lassiter took a slow turn to gather his thoughts. Victor, the bailiff, sat in the back row of the gallery. A handsome if vapid lad, he was the judge's son-in-law, and he was happy to be in uniform after flunking the police academy entrance exam twice and the firefighters' test four times.

The courtroom door squeaked open. Britt Montero, the *Miami News* reporter with the luminous green eyes, peered in, didn't find anything worthy of a two-column headline, and left. Back when Lassiter had been in night law school, having finally been cut by the Dolphins after a few undistinguished years on special teams, he had had a date with Britt, but she'd stood him up for a three-alarm fire.

He faced front. Time to crank it up again. "The evidence will show that John Deal is a building contractor of impeccable reputation who has been injured through no fault of his own," Lassiter rumbled on. "You will hear the testimony of Dr. Irwin Scheinblum, a respected physician with forty years' experience in two states."

Deal smiled to himself. Hadn't Lassiter called Scheinblum a senile, alcoholic quack who'd lost his license in Rhode Island—something about penile enlargement surgery that had resulted in a net loss—before hanging out his shingle on Coral Way? The courtroom door squeaked open again, and Deal glanced in that direction. The man who walked in looked familiar. Dark hair, short and muscular, with a mustache, a vaguely Hispanic look. Where had he seen him before?

"Yes, ladies and gentlemen," Lassiter continued. "Dr. Scheinblum will describe Mr. Deal's severe musculo-skeletal-ligamentous trauma."

In other words, whiplash.

This morning, Deal thought. I saw him this morning when I did the U-ey on Eighth Street, or whatever the hell it's called now. He was in the black Camaro right behind me. Deal turned again, stiffly, his neck flaring with pain. He squinted and envisioned the man at night, draped in a tangle of old shrimp netting, leaning on an oar on the little street running along the marina. The guy he'd almost flattened seconds before his beloved and battered Hog had plunged off the dock. What the hell was he doing here?

■   ■   ■

Jake Lassiter sipped his Grolsch and tried not to look toward the table closest to the bay. "Him?"

"Yeah," Deal said. "He's following me."

The guy sat alone near the end of the wooden deck at Scotty's Landing in the Grove. At a table next to him, two Yuppie insurance lawyers in white shirts and yellow ties were trying to score with two young women from the all-female America's Cup team.

A light breeze stirred from the east, and a three-quarter moon was rising over Key Biscayne. Jake Lassiter and John Deal were drinking beer, eating grilled dolphin, and preparing the next day's testimony.

"No, no, no! Your neck isn't simply sore," Lassiter told him. "It throbs. It aches. The pain is excruciating. Every breath is torture, every movement torment. Get it?"

"Yeah, my life is a living hell," Deal said dryly.

"That's good, John. Have you done this before?" Deal shrugged and looked toward the table nearest the bay, where the guy's face was hidden behind a copy of *Diario las Américas.*

"Could be an insurance investigator," Lassiter said, "making sure you're not doing the lambada at Club Taj."

Deal crumbled some crackers into his conch chowder. "No. He was there the night I went off the dock."

"There was a witness? Why the hell didn't you tell me?"
He studied his client a moment. "John, I may not be the
best lawyer in town, but . . ."

"Don't belittle yourself, Jake."

"No, it's true. I'm one of the few lawyers in the country
who wasn't asked to comment on the O. J. Simpson case,
even though I'm probably the only one to have tackled
him."

"For a second-string linebacker, you're not a bad lawyer, Jake, but as I recall, you usually missed tackling him."

"Thanks. But you gotta trust me now. What else have
you left out?"

Now Deal told him everything. The traffic jam that
turned into bedlam in Coconut Grove, then wheeling the
Hog down a side street, the specterlike vision of the man
draped in the shrimp net, then the plunge and crunching
descent into the black, brackish water. By the time he told
about the manatee, the old woman, and the box, it was a
three-beer story.

"What should we do, Jake?" Deal asked, finally.

"Shula would go with the play-action fake, get the corner to bite, then throw deep. But me, I just buckle up the
chin strap, lower the head, and slog straight ahead."

"What the hell's that supposed to mean?"

"Watch."

Lassiter stood and headed to the guy's table, carrying a
fresh Grolsch, a sixteen-ouncer with the porcelain stop-
per. "Hey, buddy, I wonder if you would move."

The guy glared at him and looked around. There were
no empty tables. "Move? Where?"

"Hialeah, Sopchoppy, I don't care. You're crowding my friend."

The guy stood up, barely reaching Lassiter's shoulders. He had the thick neck and sloping shoulders of a body-builder. A tattoo of a scorpion was visible on his right forearm. "My name is Hector," he said, without smiling, "and your friend has something I want very much."

"What, a personality?"

At the next table, one of the Yuppie lawyers was boasting about tossing out a paraplegic's lawsuit because the statute of limitations had expired.

"Your thieving friend stole something from me," Hector said angrily.

"Yeah, well, under the law of the sea, the Treaty of Versailles, and the doctrine of finders keepers, what he found belongs to him."

Hector grinned, but there was no humor in it. "No, *cabrón*, it belongs to me."

"Look, Hector, I'm going to count to ten, and when I get there, you're gone. One . . . two . . . three . . . C'mon, make yourself scarce. *Cuatro . . . cinco . . . seis* . . . Hey, Hector, *vete!* Seven . . . eight . . . nine . . ."

Suddenly, Hector slammed a size 10-EEE cowboy boot on Lassiter's instep. The pain shot through his ankle and radiated up his leg. Before Lassiter could recover, Hector threw a short right back, sinking it deep into his gut. The lawyer doubled over, retched, and an explosion of grilled dolphin, coleslaw, and beer showered the Yuppie lawyers.

Deal got painfully to his feet and hobbled over, but

Hector was already halfway to the dock, where a Boston Whaler sat idling, a young man at the wheel. Hector leapt into the boat, which took off, engine roaring in the no-wake zone.

Deal knelt down next to Lassiter, who was on one knee. "You look worse than I do, counselor."

"On the other hand," Lassiter said, wheezing, "there *is* something to be said for the play-action fake."

■ ■ ■

The moonlight streaked across the dark water, a highway reaching toward the horizon. A light breeze blew from the southeast, and the dive boat rocked gently at anchor. The twinkling lights of Key Biscayne condos were visible to the west. Jake Lassiter sat in the captain's chair, his bandaged foot resting inside an open cooler filled with beer and ice. John Deal removed his cervical collar and kneaded the muscles of his aching neck, then popped three Advil. It had been a long day.

"I can't believe you didn't even open it," Lassiter said.

"The old woman told me not to, said I'd be better off just to get rid of it."

"It could be jewels, drugs."

"Ebola virus," Deal added.

Lassiter shook his head. "No. It's gotta be something valuable. Why else would Hector want it so much?"

Deal shrugged and looked over the rail into the water. Seventy feet below, a Boeing 727 sat on the sandy bottom, an artificial reef for the fishermen and divers. "If the storms last month haven't stirred up everything, we'll know soon enough." In the dark water below, a light was growing brighter. "Can you trust her?" Deal asked.

"I've known Fay Leonard since she was a kid catching lobsters bare-handed off Islamorada. She's a good diver and a good friend."

"So the two of you aren't . . ."

He let it hang there.

"Ancient history, John. Ancient history."

There was a splash, and suddenly Fay was behind the boat. She spit out the regulator and slid her face mask on top of her head, and once again Deal had the powerful sense that he knew her from somewhere. It had been itching at him since they'd first met, but . . . well, it'd come to him. With her free hand, she slung a net onto the dive platform. Inside the net was a round metal canister wrapped in plastic. Lassiter hobbled toward the stern, his foot throbbing, and Deal walked stiffly to meet him. Fay came halfway up the dive ladder. "It was just where you said it would be, John, in three feet of sand just under the cockpit."

Fay pulled herself onto the dive platform, removed her tank, mask and flippers, then, without a word, peeled off her one-piece suit. She was a lithe, tanned, athletic woman in her early thirties, with sun-bleached hair tied back in a ponytail. "Jake, I'm going to take a swim," Fay said. "The water's beautiful."

"Don't you want to see what's—"

"No, you boys play treasure salvors. There's a big old manatee out there who wants some company. Just yell when you want to head back in."

She slipped gracefully into the water, the moonlight reflecting off her long limbs as she swam into the darkness. "I must be getting old," Lassiter said, " 'cause I'd rather see what's in that box than go skinny-dipping with Fay Leonard."

"As I recall, she didn't exactly invite you."

"Sure she did, John, in a woman's roundabout way."

"The way I heard it, she'd rather swim naked with a manatee."

Lassiter thought about it a moment and said, "Fay was always partial to linemen."

"C'mon," Deal said. "Let's do it."

They huddled over their prize, Deal unwrapping the plastic, Lassiter holding a flashlight. It took less than a minute. Underneath the plastic, a shiny steel canister the size of a hatbox. A wheel lock secured a door built into the top. Deal strained to turn the wheel counterclockwise. "It's stuck," he said, his face reddening.

Together they pulled, and after a moment, the wheel turned and the small door opened with a whoosh. Inside, a circle of tiny green lights immediately flashed red, and a blast of frigid air escaped. In the center of the lights, a second door with a simple slide latch led to another compartment.

"Well, counselor, here goes," Deal said.

They both held their breath. They were unaware of Fay Leonard swimming fifty yards away in the darkness, the giant manatee Booger alongside. They were unaware of the Boston Whaler with two men aboard, anchored directly in Fay's path. They were unaware of anything and everything in the whole wide world and the deep blue sea, except what treasure might rest in front of them.

Deal slid the latch and opened the interior door as Lassiter shone the flashlight inside.

"Uh-oh," Lassiter said.

"Oh Lord," Deal said.

Lassiter exhaled a tense breath. "Turn it over."

"No, you."

"C'mon. It's not alive."

"You're the ambulance chaser, Jake. You've seen stuff like this before."

"No I haven't."

Wincing, Lassiter reached into the compartment and grabbed the human head by its thick, graying hair. "It's cold," Lassiter said. "Like it's being preserved."

He turned the head over, faceup, then dropped it back into the canister.

And there it was.

Bushy beard and all.

Staring at them with wide-open eyes, a startled look on that familiar face.

The face of Fidel Castro.

THE L.A. CONNECTION

Edna Buchanan

OMENTS   EARLIER,
Britt Montero had been hungry and feverish, battling
deadlines and the blues, yearning to go home, desperate
and exhausted, her brain an overloaded computer about
to crash. But she never could resist a ringing telephone.
And Jake Lassiter knew exactly what to say.

"Have I got a story for you!"

She felt the adrenaline pump and her brain cells kick
back into life. Her blood began to tingle. She loved to
hear those words, but still, she reacted with caution.

"Have you been drinking, Jake?"

"Hell, yeah," he said. "You would be too. I've got John
Deal here . . ."

She pinched the bridge of her upturned nose and tried to ignore the distant drumbeat of an impending headache. "Isn't he the one that wrecked that entire showroom full of exotic cars . . . ?"

"Yep, that's him, he's a client of mine."

It did not surprise Britt that John Deal needed a lawyer. "Did your jury just come in?"

"No . . ."

"Then call me tomorrow."

"This isn't about him, not directly anyway." Jake lowered his deep voice for dramatic effect. "This story is so big that when word gets out, there will be riots in the streets, power grabs, and the whole damn revolution will come down."

"What are you talking about?"

"You've got to see this to believe it."

"Where are you?"

"Crandon Park Marina. Can you meet us here right away? And, uh, could you grab a couple of recent pictures, close-ups, of Fidel Castro from the newspaper morgue and bring them with you?"

"Castro? What is this? If you're putting me on, Jake . . ."

"Scout's honor, this is dead serious, in fact it could be a matter of life or death. Uh, check the wires too, before you leave. See if anything unusual is coming out of Havana."

Britt hung up and punched the send button on her computer terminal, booting into the editing system her story about the lovesick bag boy who had taken an entire

Kendall supermarket and its shoppers hostage with his father's 12-gauge shotgun.

Beyond the big bayfront windows of the *Miami News* building, the panoramic Miami Beach skyline and its twinkling lights beckoned alluringly, but she knew there was no going home soon. Her apartment on the Beach might as well have been a thousand miles away. The west drawbridge of the Venetian Causeway had been stuck in the open position since noon. On the MacArthur span, the remains of a house and several cars were scattered across the eastbound lanes. In order to save one of the last historic pioneer homes from demolition, the city had decided to move it to a new location, but the house had toppled off the wide-load flatbed and smashed into a million pieces. Several South Beach–bound motorists, startled by a house dead ahead as they ascended a fast-lane rise at fifty-five miles an hour, lost control, compounding the problem. The Julia Tuttle Causeway, two miles north, was also closed to traffic. A Hollywood movie crew had rented it for the night to shoot a high-speed chase scene for a new action epic.

Maybe Jake really had a great story, Britt thought hopefully. She loved this job. Every day was like Christmas morning. Full of surprises, stories unfolding, always the possibility that the big one would break today. So far, today had brought only two threatening letters and three obscene calls from faithful readers, while another had left chicken entrails on the hood of her new T-Bird in the *News* parking lot. She fervently *hoped* they were chicken entrails. Then came *the* assignment, followed by a major skirmish with the assistant city editor from hell.

Still steamed about the assignment, she drove south through the soft night to meet Jake, half listening to the crackle of her portable police scanner. Enthralled city, tourism, and newspaper executives were eager to cooperate with the moviemakers on location.

Final Deadline, a major action flick, would star movie hero Dash Brandon as a government agent under cover as a newsman for a major Miami newspaper. Britt's assignment, and she had been given no choice but to accept, was to help the star research his role by having him accompany her on the police beat for a week.

Unimpressed by Hollywood types, Britt resented the intrusion. But so far, the assignment hadn't been too bad, she thought, turning east across the Rickenbacker Causeway, windows open, the salt breeze bracing. The jet-lagged star wearied quickly. Summoning his limo, he had departed between the mini-riot that had broken out during a police raid on a Hialeah cockfight and the high-speed pursuit of three carloads of teenage smash-and-grabbers across the Broad Causeway from Bal Harbour.

■   ■   ■

Fay had fought hard, but Hector and Phil, despite the obvious difficulties in holding on to a slippery, wet, naked body, had succeeded in wrestling her aboard. Before Lassiter and Deal, stunned by the contents of the shiny steel canister, realized what was happening, Fay was shrieking and struggling on the deck of the Boston Whaler. Hector managed to cuff the surprisingly strong and agile woman to the handrail, but as he grinned victoriously, she landed a vicious kick to his crotch. He dropped to his knees, moaning. Phil gunned the engines, cut the running lights, and throttled into the darkness, as Lassiter and Deal collided painfully, cursing and fumbling in their haste to start the engine of their dive boat.

"Did you see that big feesh?" groaned Hector, still sitting dazed and wet on the deck.

"That shows how much you know about fishing," Phil jeered. "That was a barrel."

"It was a manatee, you jerks," Fay gasped. "Touch me and I'll rip your faces off! Who the hell are you?"

"Your friends have something that belongs to us," Hector said. "Here, cover yourself with this." He blushed and looked away as he draped something around her shoulders.

"This is a fishing net, you idiot! Where are we going?" she demanded.

■   ■   ■

Booger, buffeted about by the wake, experienced a vague sense of something amiss. It had begun as Fay flailed and grappled on the deck of the dive boat, thrashing about like a slick mermaid in the moonlight. Then he was alone, with neither a playmate nor a swimming partner. Miffed and lonely, he followed at a distance, hoping she would come back.

∎   ∎   ∎

Britt spotted Jake on the dock. The tall, sandy-haired ex–football jock was limping, and lugging a metal canister the size of a hatbox and what appeared to be a woman's one-piece bathing suit slung over his arm. The man in a neck brace who was trailing behind him had to be Deal, she thought. Both looked grim.

"What happened to you two?"

"That's not important," Jake said, wincing as he led the way. "Did you bring the pictures?"

∎   ∎   ∎

"Kidnapping?" Britt said, as they trooped into Jake's kitchen. He lived in the Grove, in a small coral rock house with no air-conditioning. They had gone there in her T-Bird after a brief but vicious argument about who would drive. Jake's foot was bandaged, and although Britt could not clearly recall the specifics of Deal's destructive swath through the exotic-car showroom, she suspected that it would be safer to skydive without a chute than travel anywhere as his passenger.

They sat at the table and filled her in on Fay's abduction.

"We have to call the FBI," she said, concerned.

"No cops," Jake said. "Bring in any kind of badge and that'll get Fay dead. I know those guys. That's why we called you."

"Jake, I'm no Rambo. What can I do?"

"Look, Britt, nobody in Miami has better contacts. We need you to check something out for us. Quietly. You'll have to sit on it for a few days, but then you'll have the story of a lifetime, and hopefully we'll have Fay back, and maybe a little something extra for our trouble."

Deal nodded and popped a handful of Advil. "Those lowlifes on the boat know who we are," he muttered. "We'll be hearing from them soon, without a doubt. We need to know who they're working for, what the hell we're dealing with here."

"They'll probably contact us, to arrange a swap," Jake said.

"Swap?"

"That's what we have to show you." Jake swept an accumulation of beer cans and pizza crusts off the cluttered tabletop and placed the metal canister in the center.

Opening the box, he lifted the lid, curling his wrists as he did so, as though unveiling a rare work of art.

The room was so hot that they could feel the whoosh of cool air, as though somebody had opened a freezer. But it was something else that prickled the hair on the back of Britt's neck. Could be it be the faint, stale aroma of cigar smoke?

Britt stared into the expressionless eyes. Fidel Castro was the man who had killed her father, stood him in front of a bullet-pocked wall on San Juan Hill and ordered his execution by firing squad when she was only three years old. "Think it's really him?" she whispered.

They could not be sure from the photos she had brought.

"Was there anything unusual on the wires out of Havana?"

Britt shook her head. "Rumors are always sweeping Miami that Castro is dead, dying, or in Switzerland having sheep-glands injections to maintain his virility."

Jake raised his eyebrows.

"Don't laugh," Britt said. "He has quite a reputation." She stared into the canister. "I've never actually seen the man in person."

"Nor I," Jake said.

"What about Magda Montiel Davis?" she said. "She'd know him." Davis, a local lawyer, had kissed Castro, gushing like an infatuated schoolgirl at a reception in Havana. She had had no inkling at the time that Cuban cameras were rolling, that Fidel would gleefully sell the footage to Miami television stations, and that enraged exiles would greet her return with threats of death, bombs, and mob violence.

All three studied the frozen face.

"What's Mickey Schwartz doing these days?" Jake said thoughtfully.

Schwartz had built a successful three-decade acting and modeling career based on the fact that he was a dead ringer for Castro. His most recent gig was a Florida lottery commercial in which he wore fatigues and blew contented smoke rings after using dollar bills, presumably lottery winnings, to light his cigar.

"This could be him," Jake said, and closed the container. "We don't want it to thaw out."

"Good thinking," Deal said.

"Maybe Castro was dying," Britt suggested, "he knew it

and wanted to be frozen until they could cure what killed him. There's a doctor into cryogenics here in Miami."

"Why wouldn't they send his entire body?" Deal said. "It would be easier to revive than finding him a whole new body."

"Maybe somebody screwed up," she said. "Remember that pop singer from Caracas? He intended to have his body frozen but there was an accident with a circular saw during the packaging. All they could salvage was his head. It's still frozen here somewhere."

"This isn't getting Fay back," Jake muttered, painfully pacing the length of the small kitchen. He paused at the refrigerator to take out a beer, and tossed one to Deal. Britt passed, no longer hungry, or thirsty. Her mind was racing. Maybe this was the big one.

"Well, I tell you," she said, after peering again into the metal container. "It's either him or Mickey Schwartz."

"Why would those guys so desperately want the head of Mickey Schwartz?" Jake asked.

They stared at one another.

"Unless they want to pass it off as Castro," she said. "Every time there are rumors of Castro's demise, Little Havana erupts. Juan Carlos Reyes has offered a million-dollar reward for proof that Castro is dead."

Reyes, a politically connected Miami millionaire, was determined to become the next president of Cuba.

"What exactly happened when they took Fay?" Britt was taking notes.

"She went skinny-dipping with a manatee."

Deal interrupted. "Do you think it could be the same manatee . . . ?"

"What?"

They told Britt the story of Deal's near-death experience and his amazing rescue from a watery grave. "Not too many manatees left these days," she said, "especially ones that would rescue a human."

"Doesn't the Navy use them?" Deal said.

"No, that's dolphins. They're smarter," Britt answered, noticing that his pupils appeared dilated.

"The old lady that pulled me out said she chats with him."

"That manatee is our only witness," Jake said. "Maybe we ought to go get the dive boat and find him."

Britt rolled her eyes. "What do you plan to do, let him sniff her bathing suit?"

Jake shrugged. "It works with police dogs."

■　　■　　■

Marion McAlister Williams was rocking in the dark on her front porch when they arrived, almost as though she had been expecting them. "He's out there," she said, nodding, "and something's wrong."

They went to the grotto. Booger was there, circling, in a state of agitation.

■　　■　　■

Booger experienced an unreasoning feeling of dread. He sensed trouble, cries for help, mortal danger. He swam as fast as he could, powerful flips of his tail propelling him southward. Dawn streaked the sky as the trio in the dive boat trailed him around a mangrove outcropping to a wooden boat dock with a million-dollar yacht appended to it.

Britt felt an odd sense of déjà vu. Like a Lassie movie, she thought, with Timmy trapped down the well.

"I know who lives here," she said, squinting at the house. "I think it's some city official."

Jake idled down the Evinrude. As they let the boat coast, they heard a splash as something hit the water.

"Hurry!" Britt cried out.

Booger dove nose-down to where a burlap bag was sinking to the silty bottom.

Burrowing beneath the sack, the gentle giant rose, bursting through the surface of the shining water, showering those aboard with spray.

"Oh, shit," Lassiter said.

If Booger had found Fay, or what was left of her, it wasn't much.

Deal reached out, caught it, then gingerly dropped the sopping sack onto the floor of the dive boat.

They gasped collectively when it moved.

Something inside was alive.

"Could be a snake," Jake warned.

Cautiously, he loosened the thick twist tie that sealed the sack. Small, high-pitched sounds emerged.

Then he upended the bag and dumped the contents onto the deck.

Six drenched calico kittens crawled in all directions, mewing loudly for their mother.

"That's who lives here!" Britt said. "The Miami Beach city manager! I should have known." The man had been seething ever since his scheme to pay bounty hunters thirty-five dollars a head to exterminate the city's stray cat population had gone awry.

"Damn," said Lassiter.

∎   ∎   ∎

Booger dove and surfaced, dove and surfaced again, then struck out for open water, as though somehow aware that he had saved the furry little creatures now using the back seat of Britt Montero's new T-Bird for a litter box.

∎   ∎   ∎

After a pit stop for Kitten Chow at an all-night convenience store, it was nearly eight a.m. Britt would only have time for a shower and a cup of coffee. She was not tired, she had never been more awake. This could be the big one, the event Miami had awaited for more than three decades. The phone rang just as she was leaving.

Hoping it was Jake with word on Fay, she felt her heart sink when she heard the deep-throated growl that had launched a thousand fan clubs. Damn, she had forgotten screen star Dash Brandon.

"You're up early," she said, trying grimly to shake off a kitten fastened by its needle-sharp claws to the right leg of her linen slacks.

"Tell you the truth, dollface, I haven't slept yet. Been partying in South Beach since I left you. You been to one a these foam parties? A trip. I met up with some of the crew, and we need your help."

"You must be too exhausted to join me today," she said, trying without success to sound regretful.

"Yeah, but we need to see you. It's important." He sounded serious. "Meet us for lunch tomorrow."

"I usually don't eat lunch," Britt said. "It's tough to eat anything on deadline." She pushed back her hair impatiently, watching a kitten dig industriously in her potted begonia. "And I'm pretty busy right now."

The movie star refused to take no for an answer. "Didn't they say you were assigned to help me?" he pouted.

5

THE OLD WOMAN
AND THE SEA

James W. Hall

ARION MCALISTER
Williams was naked in the moonlight. Her body wasn't
what it used to be. But name something that was. Especially something 102 years old. She was ankle-deep in Biscayne Bay standing in the soft marl of her own small
beach, gazing out at a prairie of moonlight that glazed the
still water. It was two in the morning on Tuesday. The
Grove was quiet, the sky was densely salted with stars,
there was no breeze, no mosquitoes, no boats moving
across the water, no birds coasting low, not even the plain-
tive warble of the owl who lived in her stand of gumbo-
limbos and strangler figs.

Marion waded deeper into the bay. The water was the

same heat as her flesh. She might have been melting into a sea of warm blood, dissolving, as she went deeper, the water to her deflated breasts, to her neck, lifting her. She lay back, let it hold her up to the moon, an offering, this woman who had seen enough of this world, what it had become, its garish pleasures, its quick and easy gratifications, its incessant noise pulsing like fevered blood. She let the tide carry her body, buoyant as a funeral pyre, let it take her out into that luminous water, so bright tonight it was as if a tablecloth of iridescent silk were floating on the surface of the bay, a cloth that was miles across.

Marion McAlister Williams was nearly the oldest thing in Miami. Older than any tree, older than any building or car or house or boat or stick of wood. She was older than the streets, older than the bridges or boardwalks or seawalls. She was older than anything but the water or the rocks or the land. Though she had to admit, one or two sea turtles still lurking in the bay might be nearly as old.

Marion drifted farther out, nearly a mile from the shore, effortless and serene, her arms spread wide, taking the last of the outgoing tide. She would float out there during the slack hour, then ride back in with the welling tide. She might have to swim a stroke or two to reach her shoreline again, but usually not. She knew the currents, the small silent streams and eddies that snaked through the bay. She knew the cycling seasons of their movements. As regular as airplane schedules, step aboard, ride out, hover for a while, and ride back in. She had been doing it for most of a century. One of the virtues of age. What you

knew, you knew well. What you didn't, no longer mat-
tered.

Ears underwater, she could hear the ripples of noise,
the subtle pings and gurgles of passing creatures. She
knew some of their names, some family lineages. There
was also a deeper sound, a nearly mystical hum in the bay
that vibrated far below the surface, a quiet throb of power
that somehow fed her, renewed her strength on these
nightly swims. She'd dared to reveal this to her granddaughter some months back, calling it a "soft drumroll of
energy," and the girl, a modern woman, skeptical and
tough-minded, had fired back that Marion was probably
only hearing the chug of sewage as it pumped from the
city's vast network of toilets and drainpipes beneath the
bay across to Virginia Key.

The slack hour passed without event, and Marion sculled the water, readjusted her body into a fast-moving
channel so she could begin her return voyage. As she
glided back toward the shore she was joined, as she so
often was, by Booger.

Tonight Booger pressed close to her, scraped her arm
with one of his barnacles, drew blood. Her skin was
papery these days, easily torn. They glided along together,
soundless, and the fleshy sea cow continued to bump her,
continued to urge her forward with something like impa-
tience. Marion did not resist. Long ago she'd abandoned
the need for overmanaging her destiny.

There was nothing she absolutely needed to do anymore. She had won her prizes, taken her bows, had
shaken the hands of a half-dozen presidents. Now her

most reliable pleasures came from these nightly rides, from giving herself over to the vagaries of the natural world. So she let Booger speed her along to the shallows just off her beach. It was there that she had made a habit of grooming Booger, clearing him of the flotsam and jetsam that he regularly snagged in his journeys around the bay.

She let her legs dangle down, caught the bottom, then trudged up to the shore, shedding water like sparkling confetti. Booger bobbed nearby, his skin silvered by the moon. Tonight he was even more of a mess than usual. He looked like a honeymoon car with strings of tin cans dragging behind him. Fishing line was wrapped around his fins, twigs and broken driftwood trapped in the line. There were two plastic six-pack holders caught on a notch near his back flipper, and knotted to them was a mooring line that trailed off behind him for twenty feet.

Marion dragged the line hand over hand, hauling the heavy mass across the soft bay bottom. It was a wonder that Booger had been able to swim at all so entangled in trash. She hauled it out of the water and held it up to the soft moonlight. Splintered wood and elastic cords and another nest of snarled fishing line that ensnared a silver canister.

Marion patted Booger, told him to wait, then walked up the shore to her chikee hut, where she kept a razor-edged fillet knife for just such tasks as this. She came back to Booger, cut him free of his clutter of trash, gave him a stroke along his broad slick forehead, and watched him turn and wallow away into the night.

■   ■   ■

Hector and Phil took Fay to their hideout. Actually, it was an efficiency apartment off Tigertail Avenue in the Grove. But Hector liked calling it their hideout even though they hadn't had to hide out in it yet, 'cause they hadn't succeeded in doing anything bad enough to be pursued.

Hector had found the apartment, liked the view of the pool, and given the manager first and last month's rent on the spot. Then he'd found he couldn't afford it, and asked Phil if he wanted to share the rent. Phil, recently split from his wife, had said sure. So they'd laid out two pool floats on the middle of the living room floor, the red one for Hector, the blue one for Phil, and called it home. Fine by Hector. Pool floats were better beds than he'd had at the Dade County Jail or Raiford. Better than when he was growing up in Havana, sleeping on the mud floor of the little barn. A goat for a roommate, chickens for companions.

This apartment was a perfect spot for spying on the babes who used the pool. Lots of them, secretaries mainly, a couple he'd gotten to know lately. Or at least he'd said a couple of words to them and given them a tongue flick. That tongue flick almost always worked on the average woman. But no luck so far with the fussy secretaries.

"Hey, man," Hector said. "I got an idea what we can do with this pretty lady she doesn't tell us what she knows."

Phil was sitting up on the kitchen counter, legs dangling. They didn't have furniture yet, so counter-sitting was about it for taking a load off your feet, except for the floats, and you couldn't use them too much or they'd spring more leaks.

Phil was staring at Fay, a weird look in his eyes. Fay was dressed in the yellow plastic foul-weather gear they'd found on the Whaler. Looking cute. Pouty lips, with some bite in her green eyes.

Hector liked women with sharp teeth, women who liked to bite. He liked teeth marks on his shoulders. He liked giving them back, a nice oval bruise on their inner thighs. Yeah. Hector had a way with women.

Phil told Hector to stop looking at Fay that way. And Hector said a very bad thing to Phil. Phil said a very bad thing back to Hector. Hector said two very bad things. And Phil replied with three very bad things.

"Knock it off," Fay said. She stalked around, staring at each of them. Hector smiling at her, trying to decide where he wanted to plant his first teeth marks.

"Now," Fay said. "Which of you idiots is going to tell me what this is all about?"

"You tell us, pussy boots," Hector said. "That's what you here for. You here to tell us whatever we ask you." Phil said a very bad thing. And Hector replied in kind.

"OK, dammit, what's going on, Phil?" Fay said. "What the hell are you doing hanging out with this creep?"

Hector spun around. "Hey, man. How come she know your name, Phil? She said your name, man. How she know that? You tell her your name, you stupid moron breath?"

Phil said a very bad thing.

Fay said, "I asked you a question, Phil."

"So did I, Phil. How she know your name, man? You know this broad?"

"She's my wife," Phil said.

Under his breath Hector said a very bad thing. Then he said three very bad things out loud.

"Ex-wife," Fay said. "Ex, Phil, ex. And this is why. This, right here, what's going on this very minute, this is exactly why you don't live at home anymore. This is why it's finished."

∎　∎　∎

Marion lugged the silver canister up to her house. She laid it on the glider on her front porch and went inside to shower and dress. Her windows were all open and the first cool breezes of the new season were sighing through them tonight. She dressed in long khaki pants and a plaid flannel shirt. She put on her brogans and rubbed some lavender-scented face cream into the grooves that lined her cheeks. She put a Band-Aid on the cut that Booger had given her.

She went back down to the porch and sat down in a wicker rocker across from the glider. Something had shifted inside her. She had felt it happen earlier. Some tectonic realignment that was sending tremors up to her flesh. She quivered with excitement for the first time in decades.

Quivering was dangerous at her age. But quiver she did. She had something in her possession that was worth something to the world at large. She sensed it. She knew that the placid young man she had pulled from the bay and nursed with Sawgrass Juice had found a similar canister and was queerly excited by its existence.

She was not sure what it meant. Canisters washing ashore? Perhaps hundreds or even thousands of silver containers drifting along the bottom of the bay. She knew she was onto something. Something of major proportions. A shipwreck out in the Gulf Stream, the canisters just now working their way to shore? Some high-tech note in a bottle thrown out from a passing spaceship? This was something new. Rejuvenating. Something that might just rescue her from the doldrums of old age.

She watched the bay brightening, saw the raspberry clouds out beyond Stiltsville, like streaks of jam across a doughy sky. She stiffened when she heard a car door slam nearby. But then relaxed, for she had recognized it. She looked out at the dawn and sighed to herself. She had made it another day. Another miracle. And now this, a second miracle. A new adventure.

She stood up, stepped to the edge of the porch. Her granddaughter was coming down the long sandy path. A beautiful young woman. Hard to believe she was carrying Marion's blood and marrow, so full of tough energy as she came striding up to the porch and halted. Her young face was seamed with worry.

"I need help, Granny."

"Not even a hello?"

"I'm sorry, I'm sorry. It's just that I'm so . . . oh, I don't know what I am at the moment. Hello, Granny."

"Hello, Fay. Now what's the matter, dear?"

But Fay was no longer holding Marion's gaze. Her eyes had shifted to the glittering canister and her mouth was working soundlessly, words without breath.

6

HEADING TO HAVANA

Carolina Hospital

NOTHER CIGAR-SMOK-
ing Don Johnson look-alike is all I need tonight, thought
Mike Weston, as he exited the 1956 Buick nicknamed El
Frankenstein by the driver. He wondered how a car could
run with so many dead parts and why Cuban government
officials were the only ones who didn't know *Miami Vice*
had been canceled ten years ago. It had taken Mike two
hours to get from the José Martí International Airport to
the house in El Vedado. This time, they had insisted the
meeting be on the island. He was told it would take place
in one of Robert Vesco's mansions, abandoned since he'd
fled the country for the safer haven of Libya.

Mike had lived in Miami for a while, so he was prepared

for his Cuba visit. Same difference, he said to himself, as he approached the front gate. This house and others in the neighborhood reminded him of those in Coral Gables, with their red tile roofs, quaint iron works, and privileged Cubans.

Robertico Robles walked in a few minutes later. Mike smiled and returned his enthusiastic handshake. Something about Robertico's slick attitude made Mike think this one would not be as easy to convince as the others. He was glad Robertico was amenable to using English. Even though Mike spoke Spanish rather fluently—one of the reasons he had been chosen for the job—he always preferred to negotiate in English. He thought it gave him the edge. They sat down in what must have been a library in the back of the house. Because of the empty shelves, their voices echoed throughout the room.

"So, Mike," began Robertico, without wasting time— something Mike found unusual in a Cuban—"what has happened to the canisters? The surgeon hasn't received them."

"I know," said Mike.

"We used your people," continued Robertico, still maintaining an almost offhand tone, "and now the goods are gone."

"I know, I know, let me explain," said Mike.

"Fidel is getting anxious. I'm not sure how much longer he'll wait before calling off the deal," Robertico said, his voice rising for the first time.

"We had an unexpected accident along the way, with a manatee—"

"A what?" interrupted Robertico.

"A manatee, you know, a sea cow," said Mike. "Anyway, we have it under control. We know where the canisters are. We just need a little more time to recover them without anyone else finding out."

"I don't know anything about sea cows, or land cows," said Robertico. "All I know is a deal is a deal and this is the second time you guys have messed up."

"Yes," agreed Mike.

Robertico was getting agitated, fidgeting with a button on his white double-breasted jacket. Mike couldn't help but notice the canary-yellow T-shirt underneath.

"When we met last month with El Maniz, he assured us this would be an easy operation," said Robertico.

It took Mike a few seconds to realize who Robertico meant by the Peanut Man: the former president who doesn't quit. The one who keeps on going and going . . .

Robertico continued, his face flushing red. "Without the head, there is no proof that he is dead. And without proof, the deal is off. Fidel will stay put. As long as his enemies know he lives, power is his only protection."

"Yes, I know," Mike interrupted. He felt the sweat flowing from his armpits. "But this is only a small detour. Most of the work is done."

"Of course," said Robertico, "especially since we supplied you with the head to begin with."

"You didn't expect *us* to do that?" Mike said, seeing an opportunity to regain the momentum. "After all, we just don't do that sort of thing in the States. Now you, on the other hand . . ."

"Sure, sure," said Robertico, waving his hand dismissively. "But let's stick to the point."

"Well, we never anticipated Castro would reject the head after we altered it."

"Of course he rejected it. There was something missing," said Robertico, lifting his cigar high in the air.

"Yes," said Mike. "But it was such a small detail. We didn't think it was important."

"Not important! Anyone close to him would have noticed," said Robertico. "The head has to be perfect."

"It will be perfect," said Mike, nodding.

"But now you have lost it."

"We'll get it back, I assure you. Give us another week," insisted Mike.

"Forty-eight hours. That's all he'll agree to. If Fidel doesn't have the head fixed and in his hands in forty-eight hours, the deal is off!" With that Robertico took a deep puff from his cigar, as if in slow motion, and walked out.

This was one tough bird, Mike mumbled to himself.

∎   ∎   ∎

Fay rushed the words out, her eyes fixed on the silver canister on the glider.

"Granny, where did you find that canister?"

The glittering object was pulling at Fay; she had seen it before.

"Booger found it in the water and I lugged it up from the beach, just now."

"You went swimming by yourself again?" said Fay, turning her attention back to Marion, who was sitting on the wicker rocker.

"You don't expect me to wait until one of you shows up, do you, dear?"

"Oh, I know, Granny, I'm sorry," said Fay, as she reached down to give Marion a kiss. "Since I opened up the dive shop, I haven't had a chance to come."

"Don't worry, dear," said Marion. "But tell me what's the matter. You look troubled."

"I need your help, Granny. But I want to know about the canister. Have you opened it yet?" asked Fay, unable to contain her curiosity. She yanked the strands of her blond hair tighter in the ponytail as she looked back at the canister.

"No. To tell you the truth," said Marion, "I was too excited to open it. But that can wait, Fay. Tell me what's wrong."

"Oh, it's Phil again," said Fay. She didn't look so tough as she rested her body against the weathered siding on the porch. The dawn's salmon hues colored everything, including Fay, with a delicate touch.

"Phil? I thought you weren't even talking to him."

"I'm not," said Fay. "It's very complicated, Granny. The bottom line is, he's gotten himself mixed up in some shady business with Cubans—he lost some merchandise he was being paid to deliver. I promised to help him, and he let me go. I know, I shouldn't have, and it's all over between us, but I think he's really afraid of these Cubans coming after him."

"Let you go?"

"It's a long story, Granny, and I'd rather not get into it."

Marion was not surprised. This would not be the first

time Fay had bailed Phil out of a jam. She remembered another time Phil had gotten involved with shady business. It had had something to do with a crooked Miami commissioner accused of accepting kickbacks from the Society for the Salvation of Sea Rigs. Phil had been one of the people caught breaking into his office attempting to gather proof. The commissioner had gotten reelected and Fay had called her to post bail for Phil. Marion remembered she had made the promise then never to get involved in her granddaughter's private affairs again.

"What merchandise?" Marion asked Fay.

"He doesn't know, but I think it might have something to do with this canister you found," said Fay, pointing to the glider.

"This canister? How can it be?" said Marion.

"I can't explain it, Granny. I just know."

"Well then, let's open it, dear."

"Yes," said Fay, as she approached the shimmering object swaying hypnotically on the glider.

Marion knew something thrilling was awaiting her. The young man had disposed of the first canister without even knowing what was inside. Now here was a second, slightly different from the first in the tint of the metal, but definitely similar. What could it be this time? She was about to find out.

Fay, too, knew this canister matched the one she had hauled out of the bay for Jake. Now she wished she had never gotten involved. But it was too late. She held her breath as she pulled the wheel lock on the top. After a few seconds, it snapped open. There was just enough morning light to make out what was inside.

"Another one," said Marion, almost disappointed-sounding. Fay, struck by a wave of nausea, found herself unable to breathe, much less speak. The air took on a red tint and she reached to her grandmother's frail shoulder for support.

"Oh dear," Marion said, struggling to steady her. "I should have warned you."

Now Fay found her voice, though she still felt ill. "What do you mean *another one,* Granny?"

"Another head. The first canister had a head in it too."

"The first canister?" asked Fay in amazement.

"The one that floated up with the young man."

"What young man, Granny? You aren't making any sense."

"The other day, I rescued a young man out of the water and he had a canister just like this one."

"But who was he? What was he doing in the water?"

"I don't know, dear. Just a nice young man who floated up on the bay. And if I'm not mistaken," said Marion, leaning over to get a better look, "his canister had the head of this same fellow."

"What do you mean the same fellow? There can't be two heads of the same fellow."

"I tell you it's the same man. I'm sure of it," Marion said. Her head was beginning to hurt, and she was feeling that vertigo she felt when she stood up too long.

"Granny," Fay said in a whisper. "Don't you know who this is?"

"No, dear, who?"

Fay told her.

"Oh my," Marion said. "I thought he looked familiar."

Marion felt the porch spin lazily around her; she was about to lose her balance. She grabbed the arms of the rocker and slowly, very slowly, put her 102-year-old body to rest. Perhaps, she thought, this was more excitement than she had bargained for.

■　　■　　■

Back in the office, Britt Montero, an emotional wreck, collapsed at her desk. She had not rested since Jake Lassiter's call. Her mind was screaming. She tried to gather her thoughts as she took a sip from her Daffy Duck Christmas mug. Coffee was the only thing she knew could calm her. She had already drunk two espressos and one café con leche at the Beach, but she needed more. Britt had served herself a mug of freshly brewed Colombian supreme blend from Publix. As she breathed in the aroma, feeling it filtering her thoughts, she wondered: Of all the reporters in town, why had Jake Lassiter called her? She wasn't the only one who could have identified that head, *the* head.

But she didn't dwell on that point. She wanted the story. She was dying for the story. Castro dead! It could lead to riots. Too much was at stake; she had to be sure.

As she refilled her Daffy Duck mug, Britt considered the loose threads, mulling over all the questions. Was this really Fidel's head? For that matter, was it anybody's head? The thing she'd seen in Jake's canister looked human to her, but maybe she hadn't looked at it closely enough. And how about the stale aroma of cigar smoke that had wafted up from the canister after Jake had opened it? Hadn't she read somewhere that Fidel had quit smoking? It was all so confusing. She needed more coffee.

Britt tossed back her wavy hair, away from her forehead; she needed to lay out a plan. The caffeine finally kicked in, and the hive on her left arm began to itch. It always itched when she was deep into a good story.

Suddenly, she decided what to do. She picked up the phone and dialed the number—a number everyone wanted and only she possessed. Just like the man whose number it was: Big Joey G., pudgy and bald, yet unassailable. Last seen coming out of the house of his private masseuse off Biscayne Boulevard. If this was as big as she thought it was, he would know something, she thought. And he owed her one.

It only took three international calls and two beeper pages for him to answer her on his cellular. He wouldn't divulge much, yet she was sure he knew more than he let on. But he did say something that jolted her. There wasn't one canister, he'd heard, there were two. And Big People were after them. He wouldn't explain any more, but he warned her to be careful.

Britt thought it was just like Big Joey G., always saying just enough, never completing the picture. That was his *modus operandi:* leave them curious.

After hanging up, Britt immediately called Jake.

"Lassiter, this is Britt. I need to see you and Deal ASAP."

"Deal is out," answered Lassiter.

"What do you mean?"

"I mean he's out. We won! The city was afraid of a big

loss, and settled his suit for nine point two million. Deal took the deal."

"Did you say nine *million?*"

"That's what I said. Anyway, he decided this other thing was a bad omen—he doesn't want anything to do with it. He left it with me and wouldn't even tell me where he was going."

"Incredible. Where was his sense of civic duty?" said Britt. "In any case, I have news for you. Can you come down to the office?"

"No, I'm too far. Give me thirty minutes and I'll meet you at the Fishbone Grill, in the Grove," said Lassiter.

"I'll give you forty-five."

Britt hung up the phone, distraught and exhilarated at the same time.

Forty-five minutes gave her just enough time to stop at the city morgue first. She had an idea. But as she grabbed her purse, the phone rang.

"Montero, *Miami News.*"

"Is this Miss Britt Montero?"

"Yes, can I help you?" answered Britt impatiently.

"Miss Montero, this is Fay Leonard. You don't know me well, but I have something to tell you. It's about—a head."

This was getting to be a busy night, Britt thought. She sat down to listen.

THE LOCK & KEY

Evelyn Mayerson

BRITT FOUND FAY Leonard in the back of the Fishbone Grill beside a chalkboard that announced Chilean salmon as the catch of the day. Except for a few grizzled men with creased and sunburnt necks speculating on the depths to which Pat Riley would ream out the Heat, the restaurant was empty.

Fay rapped her rugged nails on a polyurethane table. She and Britt knew each other slightly through their pioneer families. The difference between them was one of strata. While Fay's mother and father were able to trace their Miami roots respectively to a wrecker who had created his own wrecks by placing decoy lights and to a carpenter who had fashioned driftwood coffins, Britt's claim to founder status was only matrilineal.

"I thought it would be better," said Fay, "if we did this before Jake got here. He complicates things, if you know what I mean. It's all that busted cartilage. Whenever he moves, he clicks. It's distracting when you're trying to have a conversation."

Britt slung the wooden chair away from the table and sat astride it. "You sounded pretty frantic, Fay. What is it you want to tell me?" And weren't you supposed to be kidnapped? she thought to herself.

"My ex is missing."

"I'd say that's good news."

Fay looked around her, then leaned across the table. "This is serious, Britt. Before his disappearance, Phil told me that he was afraid that Cubans were coming after him."

"Tell him to stop renting leaky flotilla boats."

"It's nothing like that. Phil is afraid of Cuban Cubans. The last time I saw him, he was talking crazy about karate-trained guys in black shirts and some kind of business deal gone sour. I know what you're thinking, it sounded crazy to me, too. Except that what he did to me was even crazier."

The pieces of Fay's abduction suddenly came together like metal filings on a magnet. "Wait a minute. You mean it was your *ex-husband* who kidnapped you?"

Fay leaned back. "How did you find out that I was kidnapped?" Her eyes narrowed. "Of course. Jake. I should have figured. Look, Britt, it's a long story. Let's just say that I have this head that came out of a canister. And it resembles Castro. My grandmother's got it on ice, but it's beginning to thaw. She says she saw another one just like it, but I don't know whether to believe her. Old people get confused. On the other hand, I retrieved another canister myself. Whatever it's all about, it's big. Miami could lose half its population. And dummy Phil is somehow connected. I'm scared. I'm scared for Phil.''

Britt struggled to maintain a poker face, hoping that her eyebrows had not given her away. Big Joey G. was right. There really were two canisters. But that was the least of it. Britt had seen more gore and carnage than most doctors. She had heard more startling confessions than most priests. But this one had grabbed her right in the throat. It was a minute before she could make herself say anything. She wanted it to sound as hard-boiled as possible.

"People usually want to give me a story. It looks like you're here to get one.''

Fay bit open a cellophane package of oyster crackers. "I can scuba-dive to three hundred feet, Britt, but I'm over my head with this. I didn't know who else to talk to. I thought of the cops, except with Phil's rap sheet, they'll drag their feet and that could get him killed. And it all *sounds* so bizarre.''

"Can you trust your grandmother not to talk?''

"My grandmother is very closemouthed. She's kept more secrets about Miami than a scow has barnacles.''

"Exactly how do I come into this picture?''

"You're on the street, Britt. And Jake trusts you. I was hoping you would know what to do.''

Britt knew only that the safest course was to play it out,

see where it led, treat the whole scary series of events as a developing story. She collected her facts. Joey G. had also said there were two canisters. Britt had seen a head herself. Was it the same head, or were there two?

The evening was warm. Britt rolled the sleeves of her T-shirt, revealing slender yet well-muscled arms. "And a manatee found it, right?"

"Yes," said Fay. "Sort of a pet. We call him Booger. Poor guy got tangled up in it. He's always into one jam or another. The way we met, Booger swam west through a canal and got trapped in the Everglades. My grandmother strong-armed the water management people to slow the current of the canal. That's how he was able to retrace his swim back into Biscayne Bay." She paused. "Britt, how could there be *two* heads of Castro?"

"Two heads that *look* like Castro," Britt corrected. "Castro has at least two doubles."

Fay removed the rubber band from her ponytail and shook her hair free. "If you were going to kill Castro, why would you need to kill his double?"

"Maybe you didn't want his double to capitalize on his death."

"And," said Fay, "why preserve the heads in canisters?"

Britt shrugged, then stood and slung her purse over her shoulder. "Actually, when you called I was on my way to the morgue to see if there were any headless bodies."

"You think . . ."

"I don't know what I think. Follow me in your car. It's easy to find, One Bob Hope Road. You can't miss it."

Britt turned to the blackboard, picked up a piece of

chalk, and beneath the catch of the day wrote: "JAKE, MEET US AT THE MORGUE. TRY NOT TO THROW UP LIKE YOU DID LAST TIME."

■   ■   ■

Jimmy's Bronx Cafe was packed to the gills and rocking. Fidel Castro sat at the head table, threw up his hands and smiled. "Life changes," he said, and the crowd roared.

When it was over, his aides whisked him away to a stretch. He waved as the car pulled out. "I love these people," he said. "Fat cats snubbed me, true. But I took my case to the people. Angela Davis, Danny Glover, Mortimer Zuckerman, Ramsey Clark, Spike Lee, they can't all be wrong."

"And that lawyer woman. Don't forget her," said the aide beside him.

"Is she still here?"

"We can't get her to leave."

"Charm can be a burden. What about the other matter?"

"There are difficulties, *Jefe*. The cargo is missing."

"Missing? You mean like Che's hands?"

"Something like that."

"Don't talk missing! Don't use that word. It's been thirty years since Che was captured and killed. I will never forget the photograph of that beautiful, restless Argentine, the bloody desecrated stumps of his hands."

The aide felt sweat running down his shirt. "The situation of the misdirected items is temporary, Fidel. Let me assure you that we expect immediate retrieval."

"Must I do everything myself?" Fidel pounded his chest with a sharp rap. It hurt. He reminded himself of what the doctor had said, that now that he was close to seventy, chest pounding could lead to arrhythmia. Life changes, he thought.

He remembered that *The New York Times* had called him a Cold War apparition, and he sulked while the limo snaked its way through gridlock. Then he said, "I'm going to Miami."

The man next to him turned in surprise. "Fidel, *Comandante en jefe,* with all due respect, are you crazy? To Miami? How would you go?"

"The way I went before. Incognito."

"You mean the Lubavitch rabbi suit?"

"Don't be stupid. You expect me to wear that long black coat in the tropics? And you can forget about the fur hat."

"That's precisely my point. So what does that leave?"

Fidel's eyes shone. "It leaves the people. We'll do as we just did in the Big *Manzana.* By day, we'll stay in Overtown, or in Liberty City. Whatever. I'll shave my beard. By night, we'll blend. Find out the name of that Chinese restaurant I heard about in South Beach, the one with the transvestite waiters. I particularly want to see the one they call Shelley Novak. I always admired Kim Novak. For a *gringa,* she was very Cuban. You couldn't see the mustache, but you knew it was there."

Fidel Castro waved his hand. "But the most important thing is, what shall I tell El Maniz about the missing cargo? Save me from these *gringos* with their missions. If

Señor Peanut wants to get away from his wife, tell him to get a divorce. Involving himself in complicated matters of state . . ." He reached for a cigar. "If we could somehow put him together with the one who won't leave me in peace, what a pair, no?"

■   ■   ■

Jake Lassiter entered the windowless, brightly lit morgue. His swollen knee hurt. He tried not to limp. Overhead, a buzzing fluorescent was starting to go. Jake didn't know how Britt did it. He could never get used to the smell of formaldehyde or the partially masked odor of rotting flesh.

In the center of the room, Britt and Fay stood beside a metal table where a waxen cadaver lay over a trough. The women were talking to a medical examiner wearing steel mesh gloves, who was weighing a liver on a scale.

Jake brightened; the pain in his knee subsided. Attractive women and the pursuit of truth were not mutually exclusive and it was good to hone one's skills.

Fay heard him first. "Jake is coming," she said. "He's like the crocodile in *Peter Pan.*"

"I never saw the movie," said Britt. "I was too busy hating my mother."

Jake strode toward the women, then stopped abruptly, legs spread apart like the Colossus of Rhodes. He averted his eyes from the fluids running down the trough of the metal table, looked up instead at the buzzing neon light. "That's the second time you stood me up, Britt." Getting no response, he dropped his voice. It was low and husky. Women liked its sound. "You here to find a match for the head?"

Fay turned away from the medical examiner, spoke into her chest. "Heads," she mumbled. "At least there appear to be two."

Jake turned on his high-voltage Jake Lassiter laser beam stare. "No kidding?"

"But that's not why we're here. There's more."

"More heads?"

Fay's eyes glistened. "This is no time to kid around. Phil is missing."

"I hope you'd worry about me if I was missing."

"It's a human rights thing, Jake. It isn't a contest. As far as I'm concerned, you and Phil are both ancient history, so don't ask me the question you always ask, the one-to-ten scale. The answer is, as I've told you before, even when it's bad it's good."

They left the morgue after they had been assured by the medical examiner that although there were hip joints and quarter rounds washing up daily on the shores of Baker Haulover, so far there were no bodies without heads.

Jake decided on a positive approach. "We don't need the bodies. Let's work with what we have. And what we have is a couple of heads that look like Castro. Are they really Castro? Who knows? We need an ID on at least one of the heads. You can do it with photographs or dental records if you can get them, but a positive nail takes DNA."

Fay nodded her head. "We need to get an expert. Does anyone know Barry Scheck?"

"I met him once," said Jake. "At a Bar convention. It was at a plenary session on prokaryotes and nucleopeptides. But I doubt he'd remember me."

Britt fished something out of her memory. "You know Pupi Alvarez, the TV anchor? Pupi has a cousin by marriage, her name is Lilia something. According to Pupi, Lilia had a thing with Castro when she was young. She was a singer, played the Nacional Hotel before the Revolution. She met up with some of Castro's people, they took her into the mountains. Lilia didn't come down for two years. And get this, they said she kept a lock of Castro's hair."

Fay wrinkled her nose. "I thought only *santeros* did that. Why would she keep his hair?"

"It's a trophy thing."

Jake hooked his thumb into his belt. "You think she still has it?"

"Only way to find out," said Britt. "I'll put in a call to Pupi. Find out where she lives."

■   ■   ■

Surrounded by sea cucumber and spider crabs, Booger fed among the swaying, strap-bladed turtle grass. Earlier, a marine biologist had tried to entice the manatee with lettuce in order to attach a radio transmitter and a yellow float to the creature's tail. Weary of impediments, and translating the event as danger, Booger rolled out of her grasp. Now, having forgone the lettuce, he was hungry.

Booger ate his fill, including the narrow-bladed shoal grass, then swam toward shore to wait for the one in the diving mask to swim beside him and stroke his neck. He lay in the mud flats listening for outboard motors. A human with a familiar scent drifted toward him. Booger raised his snout, then wallowed toward the floating figure, discovering with a few playful taps that it was all wrong. The scent he'd known had turned, been tainted with death.

After a while, he began to toy idly with the floating thing, a bloating body whose blood had settled in the extremities and whose limbs flopped lifelessly. Weary of having to push the corpse into the currents, Booger nudged it away and continued his vigil.

∎ ∎ ∎

The crumbling neighborhood, long since severed from its purpose by a cloverleaf expressway, lay baking in the sun. A gray mockingbird darted after a spill of corn flakes from a thicket of hubcaps and vines. Even in the late afternoon, heat shimmered from the asphalt like a mirage, while an empty Metrorail car glided silently above. Over the boarded-up storefronts and empty lots strewn with torn mattresses and rusted, red-tagged chassis, hung the smell of car fumes and jasmine.

They pulled up in Fay's pickup truck in front of a sun-silvered frame bungalow. A boy in a Marlins baseball cap and high-top Air Jordans stood on a cinder block spray-painting a wall with a $2.99 can of orange Krylon.

Watching the tagger were a knot of children of varying sizes. All movement ceased as Britt, Fay, and Jake stepped down from the cab of the truck.

"Something must be gonna happen," said one child.

"Jump-outs!" yelled another.

The boy in the Marlins cap looked down in disdain from his surreal abstraction of hypodermics and coffins. "They look like undercover to you? Since when do undercover swivel they heads? More like they came to get a bump to keep them awake."

"Watch the truck," said Jake, pitching a five-dollar bill.

"Five is for the cab," said the boy in the baseball cap. "The flatbed and the aerial is gonna cost you ten."

■   ■   ■

Lilia Sands's skin was the color of vanilla. Tight black, gray-streaked ringlets molded the curve of her well-shaped skull. Wrapped in a flowered silk kimono, she had clearly once been beautiful. Now she was comely, or handsome, or whatever euphemism people assign to women who are over the hill.

Lilia Sands regarded Jake in frank assessment. "Didn't you used to play ball?"

"Linebacker."

"You look more like a tight end to me," she said.

Britt smiled, glad that Jake was getting his comeuppance, then decided to cut to the chase. "Pupi Alvarez told us that you once knew Castro."

"Yes, I knew him. It was a long time ago. I was with him in the Sierra Maestra Mountains. Hiding out from Batista's planes in ferns higher than your head, with the smell of coffee blossom coming from somewhere below."

Fay jumped in the way she dove. "Forgive the question,

but we heard . . . someone said that you and Castro were intimate.''

Lilia laughed. ''Did you ever sleep with a man on a cot? For two years? You, him, and his hobnailed combat boots? That's more than intimate. You have to be into revolution to do that.''

Fay imagined the permutations of bedding on an army cot. Jake was doing the same, while Britt maintained the ferret's focus that was her stock-in-trade.

''We heard you saved a lock of hair,'' said Britt. ''If you have it, it's very important.''

Jake intercepted the ball. ''We need it,'' he said. ''It could be evidence.''

''What kind of evidence are you talking about?''

The throb of a pumping bass rumbled from a cruising car. Britt glanced outside, then stepped away from the window. ''We can't tell you. We're asking you to trust us.''

Lilia continued to regard her visitors with a jaundiced eye.

Britt played the Latin connection card. ''Trust me.''

Lilia Sands evaluated the young woman before her, especially the tawny skin that hinted of the Caribbean. She remembered that the crime reporter had gone to bat for a former player for the L.A. Raiders by the name of D. Wayne Hudson, a friend of Lilia's son.

''I might have what you're looking for. Somewhere back here.''

Britt followed Lilia behind a tinkling beaded curtain to a bedroom with a chest of drawers. In the second drawer was a cigar box that smelled of patchouli. Lilia opened the box. Nestled in tissue paper were locks of hair of varying lengths and colors.

Lilia smiled. "I got around," she said. She raked the locks with long, well-manicured fingernails and fished out a strand bound in a red and gold Montecristo wrapper.

There was a knock at the front door.

Lilia called through the beaded curtain, "Somebody see who it is."

Jake and Fay exchanged glances. Could Hector or whoever he worked for have followed them? The rap was sharp and insistent.

"I'll get it." Tensing his body for a straight buck up the middle, Jake threw open the door.

The boy in the Marlins baseball cap and high-top Air Jordans stood on the threshold. "Where's Miss Lilia at?"

Lilia swished her way past Jake. "What's happening?"

The boy handed her a crumpled slip of paper. "Old man in cutoffs and sandals say to call this number."

Lilia turned from the boy and slipped the paper in the folds of her kimono. "It's a message," she said.

"Who from?" asked Jake.

"Garcia," she replied.

8

STRANGE FISH

Tananarive Due

ILIA SANDS WORKED
her overpainted face into a frown. "Garcia? Which Garcia? Do you know how many Garcias there are in the Dade
County phone book?" She studied the young messenger,
who was orbiting her as though he expected a tip. I'll give
you a tip, all right, kid, Jake Lassiter thought. You'd better
earn that ten bucks I just gave you and go back outside to
keep an eye on Fay's pickup.

"What's his first name?" she asked the boy.

He shrugged. "He said you'd know."

Lilia smiled, then delicately raised her fingertips to her
temple as if to brush away imaginary perspiration.

"Ah . . ." she said, with a long, rapturous sigh. *"That Garcia."*

Jake shifted his weight from one sore leg to the other. Time out, he thought. He, Britt, and Fay had come to Lilia's for a lock of Castro's hair—the *real* Castro's hair. So, they had what they'd come for. No need to tango here all day. Even a pit bull reporter like Britt had to know when it was time to move on.

"Look, Miss Sands," he said, surprised at his own politeness, "we can bail out of here if you need to catch up on your phone calls."

"This will interest you," Lilia said, holding up her index finger to silence Jake. (Watching, Fay and Britt both took mental note of this tactic in case it might come in handy someday.) Lilia cradled the receiver of her black novelty telephone, which was shaped like a baby grand piano. Each time she pressed a key, a tone sounded; she was dialing a laborious version of "When the Saints Go Marching In."

Long-distance, Britt noticed.

Off key, Fay decided.

Damn annoying, Jake thought.

"It's me. Put him on," Lilia said abruptly, in Spanish, and then she smiled and nodded, her green-flecked brown eyes wide with pleasure as she listened to an indiscernible voice. Hanging up, she surveyed her waiting audience as though she were reliving a finale number onstage at the Nacional.

"I shouldn't tell you this . . ." Lilia began.

But you will, Britt thought, perking up. Sentences that

began with "I shouldn't tell you this" were verbal foreplay, and satisfaction was never far behind.

"You didn't hear this from me, and don't ask who told me—but Miami is about to have an important visitor from Cuba. Believe me, when *he* comes, the people's reaction will make Nelson Mandela's reception in Miami look like the papal visit. He's coming soon, within days. He didn't say exactly when."

"Give me a break," Jake said, not buying it.

"It can't be," Fay said.

"It is," Lilia said, beaming.

Britt's brain was turning somersaults. Not one head, but two, and Fidel was *still* alive? And, apparently, intending to set foot in a city that nourished itself on fantasies about the day he would drop dead? Home to weekend commandos who would love to help him do just that, with a million-dollar price tag on his head?

Castro is Coming! Britt was already thinking in headlines. This was top-strip, front-page, WW II type. She'd need to get on the phone and pull some favors with her sister-in-law's bureaucrat uncle in Havana to get confirmation.

Britt's delight at the whiff of a huge story warred with her disappointment that the man who killed her father was still breathing. "I can't believe he's alive," she said.

"*Sí, cómo no,*" Lilia said. "Of course he's alive. But if he's planning to come to Miami, he's obviously lost his head."

Silence. The three of them started.

"What do you mean?" Britt asked first.

Lilia circled her finger around her ear. "You know . . . *loco.*"

The proportions of this story were growing in light-years, Britt realized. They'd been fearing riots if people thought Fidel was *dead?* What about the riots when word got out that he was about to enjoy a big plate of arroz con pollo in the glare of fluorescent lights and mirrors at La Carreta?

Did that phone call mean that this woman, a disenchanted revolutionary, was still maintaining her own special brand of diplomatic relations with Fidel Castro? And if that was the case, exactly how "inside" was her mysterious tipster on the phone?

Britt, having a hunch—and her hunches were rarely wrong—fixed a probing gaze on Lilia.

"Listen," Britt said, "on a scale from one to one hundred, if I ask how confident you are of that tip—how close your source is to Castro himself—where would it rank? Tell me that and we'll be out of your life."

Lilia smiled a wide smile. She was reliving memories that had wiped thirty years from her face; there was no mistaking that despite politics, she was in love.

"One hundred and ten."

Right again, Britt thought. Fidel had been on the phone.

Guess who's coming to dinner, Britt told herself, already writing her story's lead in her head.

"Doesn't make sense," Jake said, holding the door open for Fay and Britt as they walked outside into the liquid afternoon heat. His hulking form stood high above the two women. "If Castro comes here, Miami's welcoming committee is going to grind him into hamburger. Or picadillo anyway. He won't last two hours."

"Maybe that's what he wants," Britt said. "Think about it. Phony heads. A staged assassination. A reward for proof of his death. And where better than Miami? Everyone *expects* people to get killed in Miami."

Fay, following them to the curb, was silent. She noticed that her pickup was now tagged KING in bright orange paint across the cab, and the kid had vanished. Jake cursed loudly, but Fay wasn't worried about her truck. She had other things on her mind.

There was no mistaking that Pulitzer lust glazing Britt's eyes, so Fay figured her friend would head straight for the newspaper, where she'd be no help—and Jake was content, saying something about getting a beer. Him and his damned Grolsch. It figured. He'd always been too eager to punt on fourth down instead of going for it, she recalled from their brief courtship.

To her, something just didn't add up. Even if those creepy Castro heads were part of some fake assassination scheme, how had one of them found its way into her grandmother's hands by way of Booger, the manatee? And they still weren't any closer to figuring out what had happened to Phil, her ex-husband, who'd been mixed up in bringing the heads in the first place.

It would be funny if it weren't so pathetic, Fay thought. She could have told whoever had hired Phil that the guy couldn't be trusted to bring back the change from the grocery store, or even the groceries, much less deliver valuable cargo.

The poor jerk had already tried to kidnap her to get the

heads back once he lost them, and now they'd somehow led to his disappearance. He was a loser, but he was *her* loser, and it had touched her to see him so shaken. Her stupid mothering instinct had drawn her to Phil in the first place, like a moth to a burning stick of dynamite. She should have listened to her grandmother and gotten a puppy instead, and she wouldn't be in this mess now.

Granny.

A thought made Fay shiver slightly, despite the hostile midafternoon sun: If Castro's heads had put Phil in danger, wasn't her grandmother in danger too?

Granny had tucked the lone metal canister with Castro's head on the bottom shelf of her refrigerator—"Just in case it starts to thaw," she'd said, patting it like a leftover pot roast. "I'm not too fond of dead flesh at room temperature, Fay. Even a head of state."

Fay wasn't crazy about dead flesh at any temperature, especially disembodied flesh. As soon as she got to a phone, Fay decided, she would give her grandmother a call, just to hear her voice. That way, maybe she could shake off the feeling, which had snaked its way around her middle, that something was terribly wrong.

■　　■　　■

It was a body.

Fishing off the bay at Peacock Park in Coconut Grove on Sundays, all day on Sunday, standing on the same spot of fine white sand beside his favorite clump of sea grape trees, Vernon Sawyer had seen enough floaters over the years to know one from a distance. And this one was bobbing only fifteen yards out, just beyond his plastic red and white cork, a patch of unexpected shade for a school of minnows that had just vanished underneath it.

That was the thing about this park, which seemed to Vernon like a tiny strip of paradise for the common man. There was more to it than the neatly planted rows of coconut palms, or the view of the legion of rich folks' sailboats docked across the way. You never knew what you would find here, whether it was a squatters' campsite built from plastic wrapped around a trio of palm trees or an unforgettable conversation with a vagrant who'd seen the world and who understood its workings, inside his unkempt head, better than any coiffed, overfed politician he might ever meet.

That was why Vernon came here, for the surprises. It sure wasn't for the fish.

Today's surprise, the body, was fairly fresh, hardly any swelling, not puffed the way bodies get when they've been in the water for days. Once, Vernon had seen a brother who'd ballooned so big that his skin had peeled off white, except in spots.

Not this one. Not her.

It was a woman, a white lady, he could see that. She looked almost serene, bobbing facedown in the rust-colored water as though she were embracing it. Her white hair fanned around her head like a lace wedding veil. Her lifeless body was clothed in a pair of soaked khakis and a dark shirt, maybe plaid.

Shame, Vernon thought. She'd preserved a quiet dignity like this, floating undisturbed, never mind the empty water jug and plastic bag drifting beside her. Soon, with all of the flashing sirens and strangers' hands pulling on her, probing her, she'd be just another corpse. Her spirit might be at rest, but her body's work for the day had just begun.

The current was lulling her and her entourage of trash toward him, so Vernon decided to fish her out himself. He was a fisherman, after all, even if all he used was a cane pole baited with bread, and even if he couldn't remember the last time he'd caught anything living. He wasn't afraid to touch bodies; they were just vessels, more or less, like the empty Coke bottles and crushed cigarette packages strewn across the water's edge.

Vernon yanked his line out of the water, and his suspicion was confirmed. The bait was long gone. Some crafty little bugger had taken it without so much as a ripple. Anyone who doesn't think fish are as smart as people don't know many fish, Vernon thought.

He cast the line out as far as he could, aiming for the back of the dead woman's shirt collar, then gently pulled on it to see if something would catch.

Something did. He must have snagged her skin or clothing, because the line went completely taut when Vernon pulled. He'd have to stand up for this one, he decided. Even an old woman's body, waterlogged, weighed much more than he'd counted on.

By the time the cane pole snapped in half, the body was close enough for Vernon to wade out and grab the pudgy, lifeless fingers. "Thatta girl," Vernon mumbled, gripping her tight to guide her from her floating grave.

Rolling the corpse over, breathing just a bit hard from the ordeal, Vernon almost didn't recognize her at first.

She was more bloated than he'd thought, her face roundish and smoothed nearly free of the most familiar wrinkles. And the eyes he'd known had always flickered and danced; he'd never seen these cloud-gray dead eyes on this particular face before.

Strange as it was, the first thing he recognized was the smile. It was the same one he'd seen nearly every Sunday for ten years; the ready, thin-lipped smile that had brought them from being strangers to damn near being friends who shared only a love for the park. Friends enough that he'd warned her time and again about swimming out here by herself, a woman her age, old enough to be his mother. And friends enough that he had to swallow back hard and clamp his teeth shut when he realized that even though the smile was still there, his friend was long gone.

"Darn you, Marion," he whispered, brushing a glistening gum wrapper from her matted hair. "What've you gone and done now?"

■ ■ ■

Fay didn't want Britt to hug her too long, because then the comforting numbness of the shock might wear off, and she wasn't ready for that yet. Right now, she felt like she was in the middle of an elaborate movie scene at the edge of the bay, and the stunt double for her grandmother, entombed in a black body bag inside of the ambulance beside her, was the victim of some freak accident on the set. That fantasy was almost keeping her from shaking at all.

"Kid, I'm so sorry," Britt said. Then, instinctively, Britt knew she had to snap out of human mode and let her machinery take over. Poor Fay wouldn't be any good to her if she crumbled into an emotional wreck. Marion Mc-Alister Williams had been much more than Fay's grandmother; she was the whole city's surrogate guardian, its conscience, and now she'd been found dead as if she'd been choked by the trash she'd decried for so long. Everyone would want answers, and Britt had to find some fast.

Britt paused, her pen in midstroke from scribbling wildly in her notebook. Between the impending Castro visit and Marion McAlister Williams's sudden death, she was juggling two huge stories, possibly three, depending on what was going on with those heads. Should she phone her editor for backup?

Yeah, right, she thought. "What did the police say to you?" Britt asked Fay, regaining her senses.

"They aren't saying much," Fay answered in a hollow voice. "All I know is, a fisherman pulled her out of the water about an hour ago. That guy over there. He's giving a statement."

"Do you think she went swimming?"

"Not with her clothes on. No way. She's the one who taught me, 'It's naked or nothing.' Britt, I'm thinking . . ."

Britt nodded. "I know. It's connected to the Castro heads. I'm thinking the same thing. So's Jake. He's already headed for her house. We're all over this. Don't worry."

Suddenly, something broke through Fay's frozen

thoughts to bring her attention to the water. She'd seen something moving out there, something big. Another body? Had her grandmother's murderers killed Phil, too?

But when she saw the dark gray head pop out of a wake, she realized it was only Booger. He was everywhere, like a swimming spirit guide. Booger had probably been witness to the whole horrible business from beginning to end. All of the answers were right there behind those doleful, dull black eyes. If only manatees could talk . . . At least Flipper could splash and make frantic chattering sounds, Fay thought. Eventually, the kid and his dad had always figured it out: Danger. This way. Hurry.

With Booger, nothing.

Then Fay felt the shock thinning. Her grandmother was gone. "Britt," she said, barely a whisper. "I've lost her."

Britt stared at her friend's wide, wondering eyes, framed by strands of blond hair blown across her forehead. For the first time in a long time, Britt couldn't think of a snappy comeback.

"Um . . . excuse me. Miss, are you Marion's granddaughter?"

It was the black fisherman, shading his eyes from the glare of the sunset with one hand as he stood before them, his features grim. Gazing at the dark, tallish man with salt-and-pepper hair, Fay realized she'd seen him around, fishing with a bamboo pole.

Fay could only nod.

"You're the one who found her," Britt said. "Boy, do we need to talk to you. Hope you don't mind."

"Don't mind a'tall," the man said, smiling sadly. "Mar-

ion was a fine, fine lady. I'm just so sick about the circum-
stances. Always told her to be careful, but I never in a
million years expected her to drown. Not Marion."

"She didn't just drown," Fay said with certainty.

"That's why we have to ask you questions. We're sure
she had some help."

The man's face went slack with surprise. "You don't
say? Well, I'll be damned. The police didn't say anything
like that, about a murder. In that case, I hope I haven't
made a mistake. I guess I've been holding on to something you might call evidence."

"What do you mean?" Britt asked.

The fisherman looked nervous, glancing back toward
the police officers crowded around the open ambulance
door. "Well . . . I didn't think it was right to give it to
them. I wanted to wait for someone from the family.
Thought that would be the proper thing."

"What?" Fay asked.

"You see, miss . . . I know Marion was dead when I
pulled her out of the water. I took her pulse to be sure,
but I knew. Even the police say she'd probably been in
there some time, maybe a full day. But when I found her,
she had the tiniest smile on her face. You can't see it now.
It was gone, last I checked. But we were friends, your
grandmother and I. This might sound funny, but it was
like she'd saved that smile for me. And after I pulled her
out, I was sitting beside her, looking at her, sorry she was
gone, when I felt something land on my hand."

Seeing their rapt faces, the fisherman looked slightly
embarrassed. He averted his glassy eyes. "I figured the
police would lock me in a nuthouse if I told them this

next part. Your grandmother's hand had moved, dropped on top of mine. And she was still dead as could be. That's the gospel truth. I looked down, and her palm was wide open. I don't know how she did it, but she'd been holding on to something, and it was right there in her hand. It was like she wanted to make sure I would find it. I knew it must be important."

With that, the fisherman gently reached for Fay's wrist, holding her palm upright, and pressed his hand into it. As Britt leaned over to stare with unbridled curiosity, Fay felt something tiny, sharp, and slightly cold pass from the fisherman's callused hand to the soft of her palm.

"Take it," he said. "I'm sure it must be for you."

9

SOUTH BEACH SERENADE

Brian Antoni

FAY SQUEEZED THE object in her hand as she felt a tidal wave of emptiness wash over her. She tried to calm herself by staring into the fisherman's kind eyes as she felt her own eyes start to water, and she thought how water, this water in front of her, had been her Granny's life. The fisherman hugged her, as he whispered into her ear, "She wanted to go, child, anyone who dies with such a sweet smile on her face wants to go."

Fay knew what was in her hand. She didn't even have to look at it. She shoved it into her pocket. She knew what she had to do, but it would have to wait until tomorrow.

The door to Marion's house was unlocked, as usual.

Everything looked as it always had. She went straight for the refrigerator and opened it. Two Joe's take-out containers, a half-empty bottle of prune juice, a head of lettuce in a bag marked "Booger." And a big empty space in the middle. No canister.

The phone rang. She picked it up without saying a word. After a minute, she said, "Jake, the head's gone."

Jake put down the phone and sat down at the kitchen dinette, stared at the canister on the table, wondered how long before they came for this one, too.

∎　　∎　　∎

John Deal sat on the Havantur bus, thinking of how long he'd dreamed of the day he could buy a big Hatteras and live happily ever after in the Bahamas. Now that his dream had come true, he suffered from an overload of fun, sun, rum, sex, drugs, suffered from too much marination in gin-clear salt waters, his head like an olive in a martini. He felt trapped in a picture postcard, paradise-overdosed. He'd come to Havana to try to snap himself out of it, get a shot of reality. The tour guide, whose name was Dogma or Dagma, spoke English with a heavy Russian accent. Deal couldn't understand anything she said. He gave up when she pointed to a pineapple finial on a rooftop and said, "The pineapple resides on that edifice because it's the symbol of tropical fruit."

As they drove around the city, John Deal got more and more depressed. I didn't need this much reality, he thought. It was like driving through South Miami after Hurricane Andrew. Buildings, some of the most beautiful he had ever seen, were in ruins. Everyone seemed dazed, like zombies.

The bus stopped in Havana Viejo. Deal trailed the walking tour, looking into the almost empty stores. An emaciated old black woman said out of the corner of her mouth, "If you're a reporter, tell them we're starving," and kept walking. Prostitutes in spandex with badly bleached hair called out to him. Some of them looked so young, like little girls masquerading as whores for Halloween. Hustlers harassed him, asking him what he needed. Cocaine? *Putas? Muchachos?* He answered, *"Nada, nada, nada."*

Deal couldn't deal with it anymore. He craved a drink or two or three, as he stumbled on La Bodequita del Medio. The bar of the cavelike restaurant was covered with graffiti and pictures of Hemingway. He wondered if there was any bar in the world where Hemingway hadn't drunk. He read a sign that said "Home of the Mojito," so he ordered one, as a tough-looking young man dressed like Dick Tracy walked over and sat next to him at the bar. "I'm Mike Weston from Miami," he said, holding out his hand. John shook it.

"You here for the babes," Mike said, "right?" John just looked at him. "Havana is the best place for *putas* in the world. In Miami," Mike went on, "chicks think they're too good for you even if they're dogs. In Cuba, for five dollars you can get Claudia Schiffer. And they're pure. They don't got AIDS. Any fifteen-year-old chick can be yours for five dollars. Some only want soap."

Deal tried to imagine being desperate enough to have sex with someone who only wanted to get clean, wondered how long the embargo would last if the Miami Cubans knew what it was doing to their own people.

"Got to go now," Mike said, leaving to join a group of men who had just entered the bar. They sat at a table in the back surrounded by Cuban soldiers.

Deal rubbed his eyes. One of the guys looked like Juan Carlos Reyes, that deluded rich guy who thought he was president of Cuba in exile. He was sure the pudgy bald guy at the head of the table was Big Joey G. One other guy at the table looked familiar.

Deal tried to place him as he tossed back another mojito, and then it hit him. It was that Cuban guy, Hector, in Miami. The guy who'd forced him off the road into the bay, then followed him around when he had the head. Hector didn't look too thrilled about being with this particular group. And there was a pasty-faced Anglo-looking guy beside him who looked just as unhappy.

Deal faced dead ahead now, shaking his head, sipping his drink. He was gonna sit there till they left. He didn't want to be recognized. Time went by in slow motion. Then Deal felt a tap on his shoulder. His heart stopped. He turned around. It was Mike Weston. "Hey, man, you want to come with me and score some Schiffers?" he asked.

∎　∎　∎

Lilia Sands sat in her house in Overtown, on her plastic-covered velvet settee, the one that no one was allowed to sit on. She was dressed in her favorite nightgown, the one with the silk and feathers and lace, the one she called her wedding dress, the one she wanted to be buried in. Light from the huge moon over Miami flowed through the window. There was something in the hot air. Lilia could feel it, could taste it. It was the tropics; it was her youth; it was Cuba. She was sure the air she was breathing had blown up from her beloved Cuba. Her fingers stroked her guitar.

Lilia drifted back, flowed with the air back to Cuba, back to the day her parents had given her to the nuns because they had no food to feed her because of Batista, back to the day the nuns had shaved her head, and taken her one dress, the one made from the train of her mother's wedding gown. She'd sat naked in front of the convent window, tears streaming down her face as she touched the luxurious pile of black hair on the floor that would soon be made into a wig, unable to make herself put on the coarse black habit. She remembered caressing her long swanlike neck, her perfect soft breasts, her hand following the flow of sweat down, caressing her belly, touching the only hair she had left. But before she could escape into herself, a cold, hard hand had clapped over her mouth. She'd tried to scream but nothing came out.

■　　■　　■

As the man in the trademark olive fatigues bounced along Miami's potholed Overtown streets in the back of the white stretch limo, he strained to remember. He wanted to get the details perfect by the time he arrived at Lilia's house: He had seen her in the moonlight, an image so beautiful that it hurt, causing a throbbing pain in his groin. She'd looked like some kind of angel, some kind of Madonna, some kind of whore sitting in the convent window. She was everything, she was nothing, she was Cuba. And as Columbus had said when he landed on the island, "No man has ever seen a land as beautiful as this." No man had ever seen a woman as beautiful as Lilia. He couldn't help himself. He'd stripped off his clothes, his body the white of sweet condensed milk, hard, trembling with anticipation. He'd climbed the statue of the Virgin de la Caridad del Cobre, grabbed a rose trellis, not even feeling the thorns of the rosebushes cutting into his skin, and left tiny dewdrops of red blood on the white windowsill as he climbed into Lilia's room.

■　　■　　■

Now the limo was passing the vacant lot beside the small house where Lilia lay back on the settee, strumming the guitar, singing to her memories, to the moon.

Lilia remembered that at the exact moment she had felt the hand on her mouth, she had felt the lips on her bald scalp, then a warm tongue licking, licking, licking like a kitten licking cream. And with each lick she'd melted with pleasure, so much pleasure that she knew in her heart that there was nothing she wouldn't do for this nameless, faceless man. And he'd removed his hand from her face to swallow her mouth with his and he'd tasted of the brown caramel sauce on flan. Then he'd pulled away from her and held out his arms and he looked like Jesus on the cross, those same suffering eyes and the blood dripping from his rose-pricked body, and he'd said, "I,

Fidel Castro, on this Good Friday in the year of Our Lord one thousand nine hundred and fifty, will turn you, my queen, into a woman and will begin my destiny of turning Cuba into a real man, one that would never starve his children."

And then Lilia remembered how Fidel had taken her in his arms and laid her down on the hard little nun cot and it was like it was made out of the finest down, and then, Dios mia, sweet heart of Jesus, he entered her, the intense pleasure-pain of it, and the nuns broke out into a chorus of "Ave Maria," and birds started to sing even though it was nighttime, and all the glass in the convent shattered and the rosebushes pushed out such a rose smell that spread throughout the island, causing all the men in Cuba to grow with desire and all women to weep with satisfaction. He made love to her for three days and three nights and when he tried to leave she grabbed his hair and bit his left earlobe, taking a notch of flesh between her teeth, tasting his blood. But his strength was too great. As he finally broke free and his hair gave way, she was left with a lock in her hand and a piece of his ear in her mouth.

Lilia heard the churn of the limo's big *gringo* engine as it stopped in front of her house. She dropped the guitar and rose to her feet, drawn up by some unseen force. Outside, the sunroof of the limo slid open and he sprang through, like a jack-in-the-box, like a God lit up by a shaft of moonlight, and at the exact same time, the candle she was burning to Ochun flared.

Lilia felt her feet start to move before she could even think, and she was out the door, in the street, and she entered and he was there, her love was there and beautiful and the years had been kind to him and she could hardly breathe as he said, "I told you I would come and get you in a giant white chariot." Then somehow her nightgown melted off her body, the feathers detaching and fluttering around her. The only thing she could do was say his name, the most beautiful word in the world to her, "Fidelito!" Her whole body trembled as he brought his lips to hers and took her in his arms. And then, nothing. Something was wrong. No taste of caramel. She stroked his hair, started to cry for their lost youth. As she cried, she reached out to touch his left ear, then to caress it. It was smooth, whole, unscarred.

Lilia jerked up wildly, shoving with animal fury, shrinking from him as if he had opened his mouth and revealed a serpent's tongue.

When she finally found her voice she screamed, "Fraud! Where's my Fidel?"

∎   ∎   ∎

Britt was going to give her lunch appointment with Dash Brandon two chances: minuscule and infinitesimal. If she couldn't find a parking space on Ocean Drive, she would drive right by Brandon without a glance in the rearview. She'd come up with some excuse later. Her computer crashed on deadline. The causeway bridge got stuck open. Her cats ate her homework.

But just as she passed the corner of Ninth Street, a pink and white '56 Chevy convertible glided out from the parking spot it had occupied since the Reagan administration, forcing Britt to slam on her brakes less than a block from the News Cafe, where Dash awaited. She glanced suspiciously at the gaping vacancy on the curb directly opposite her. She hadn't seen that much real estate by a parking meter in South Beach in months.

"What the hell," she sighed, and pulled in. From a table on the terrace, Dash and a plump man wearing a dog collar, tight leather pants, and a T-shirt that said "SOBE, where the girls are strong and the men are pretty," watched South Beach's human smorgasbord parade past the News Cafe: models and more models, male and female, the greatest concentration of beauty that had ever occurred in the history of the planet; old retirees and young ultratrendies dressed in the same "vintage" outfits; struggling artists splattered in paint; real estate agents frothing at the mouth; tattooed Mariel refugees smoking cigars; punks with red hair, old ladies with blue hair; European backpackers; Eurotrash; topless-G-string beauties baking brown almost all over; greased muscle-bound depilated gay boys; Hasids in fur hats and black coats; Miami gangbangers; pimps; whores; celebutantes; dominatrices. The parade was framed by blowing coconut palms, warm white sand, sparkling sea. Windsurfers, Hobies, Cigarettes, yachts, cruise ships, and sun-bleached surfers skimmed by on the ocean. Pelicans, Frisbees, wild parrots, seagulls, blimps, kites, and airplanes pulling advertisements flew by in the sky.

As the remnants of last night's Special K drug dripped from his brain, Dash swallowed down big spoonfuls of Special K cereal. He licked his lips, could not keep his eyes from the bouncing breasts. His companion inhaled his coffee and cigarettes, stared transfixed at the bulging men's baskets. Britt walked up to their table; Dash jumped up, kissed her on both cheeks, and pulled a chair for her.

"This," Dash said, introducing her to Ziff Bodine, "is the best special-effects man in the business."

Ziff, Britt noted, either was wearing black nail polish or had recently slammed both hands in a car door.

"The most valuable prop for his film is missing, stolen," Ziff blurted. "It would take me weeks to reproduce," he whined. "If we're going to stay on schedule—"

"What is it?"

"Fidel Castro, his head actually."

Britt spit up her coffee and stared at the man.

"Is it . . . very lifelike?"

Ziff leaned back in his chair, mouth open in surprise. Then he smirked.

"Lifelike?" His eyes shifted to Dash. "She wants to know if it's lifelike." He leaned forward. "Did you see *Alien Autopsy*? That was my work. I did that."

"It *better* be lifelike," Dash sneered. "It cost enough."

Somehow these clowns had gotten wind of her situation, Britt thought. Had to be some elaborate joke. But Dash leaned across the table, his big hand on her slender arm. The man gave her the creeps. She'd always hated to watch him on the screen and he wasn't revising her thinking much in the flesh.

"I had a call on my answering machine this morning. A woman's voice. She said if I 'wanted my head' I better show at Paulo Muschino's house tonight for dinner. I want you to go there with me."

Britt wasn't sure she believed Dash had really gotten

any message like that, and even if he had, it might be some kind of lame publicity stunt. And the last place she wanted to be was at some trendoid South Beach party on Dash's arm. But at this point, mention the word "head" and Britt was there.

"I'll come, Dash," Britt said. "But this better not be some sicko come-on."

■　　■　　■

As the limo cruised through the South Beach evening, Britt thought how much she hated it; drecko sandbar turned vulgar freak show, excreter of endless hype, festering petri dish of sexual disease and perversion, a sure sign of the apocalypse. "What do you think," Britt said snarkily, "they're going to serve the head as a main course?"

Dash ignored her. "Isn't South Beach the coolest?" Dash said, as the limo pulled onto Ocean, a honky-tonk on XTC, and stopped at Maison Marzipan.

"Isn't Muschino the coolest?" Dash said, as they walked into the fake Italian palazzo owned by the real Italian. Britt remembered when it had been a low-rent apartment building filled with friends of hers, struggling writers and artists.

"His clothes are the coolest," Britt said sarcastically, thinking they only looked good on call boys.

A butler, naked except for white gloves and a Muschino scarf wrapped around his waist, led them through rooms that looked like a vulgar Hollywood version of Pompeii. They passed through a walkway filled with fake Greek urns, into the dining room filled with fake Chinese silks. Everyone stopped talking, looked up. Paulo air-kissed Dash on both cheeks, ignored Britt. "You're here just in time for dessert," Paulo said, sitting Dash next to him, motioning at Britt with a flick of his hand. She was seated at the other end in table Siberia, between a sexless, no-talent writer and that lesbian fox Antonia Cesare. Next to Antonia was Madonna, who was in a liplock with that vapid bitters heir Chris Angostura.

Paulo was talking to Claudia Schiffer. "I don't understand," he said, waving his wineglass dismissively. "What it is you date? A magician? What he do? Pull rabbits out of hat?"

"So what was for dinner?" Britt asked, picking up the engraved menu. " 'Boiled loggerhead turtle eggs,' " she read aloud. " 'Florida panther steaks with béarnaise. Manatee mousse.' "

"It was a Florida theme dinner in honor of Marion McAlister Williams," Madonna said. "She just died, or something."

A gong rang and Paulo stood up. "Now for dessert, the most endangered species of all, the South Beach virgin." A flawless naked black girl, covered in melted white chocolate and surrounded by fresh fruit, was rolled out on a silver tray at one end of the table, while at the same time a flawless naked white boy covered in dark chocolate and surrounded with fruit was pushed out at the other end. Dash picked up a peeled banana from next to the girl, giggled, and asked, "Where should I dip it?"

The white-chocolate confection opened her mouth,

the icing cracking as she said, "If you want head, go to Hell."

∎   ∎   ∎

Thousands of people holding VIP invitations to the grand opening of a new nightclub named Hell were frenzied; screaming, begging, crying, rushing the velvet ropes. Hundreds of oversteroided bouncers held them back. Dash and Britt got out of the limo to the cry of "Dash! Dash!" Cameras flashed. The crowd parted, like the Red Sea for Moses. The velvet ropes lowered and they walked up the red carpet into Hell.

Britt felt the darkness devour, the heat hit, the beat throb. Fog filled the room. Red and blue spotlights spun and twisted as green lasers pierced and wiggled the darkness, then turned into wheels and spun. Dash led her through the sea of flesh, torsos and trunks, heads and tails, which rose in tiers from the dance floor. Everyone was in a different stage of undress, showing off tattoos and body piercing. Some were completely naked. Every variety and possible combination of sex was taking place. A woman wearing an Astroturf dress grabbed on to a speaker as she was mounted from behind by a man covered from head to toe in leather.

Britt felt faint, like she was swimming. Then she looked down and saw sharks, big ones, gliding in a floodlit subterranean aquarium under the glass dance floor beneath her feet. Just then a woman pushed up to them, held open her coat, a walking drugstore, and asked if they wanted speed, XTC, LSD, GHB, smack, crystal mesh, poppers, barbs, coke, rock, Chat, 'shrooms, peyote, opium.

"You got any sugarless gum?" Britt asked.

Outside the ropes the crowd was getting more and more unruly, as Juan Carlos Reyes arrived with two dozen members of the First of April anti-Castro paramilitary group, tipped off by an anonymous phone call that an extremely high official of the Cuban government was going to be at the opening.

Inside, the main stage of Hell was flooded with light. Shelley Novak led a chorus line of drag queens. In her hands she held a silver platter, sautéed in blood, topped with an extremely lifelike head of Fidel Castro.

"There's my damn prop!" Dash said, pointing to the head, pulling Britt in his direction. As they lurched forward in the throng, machines started pumping foam all over the club as the revelers cried out in unison.

The din was so great nobody even heard the commotion at the door when the bouncers refused to let Juan Carlos and his men in. At Reyes's signal, they butted the bouncers with their guns and stormed in. The crowd of thousands still waiting outside the velvet ropes saw their opportunity and rushed behind them, screaming, into the club, into the darkness, the heat, the smoke, the foam, onto the dance floor all at once. Onstage, a conga line of fifty Castros in tutus kicked in unison. Juan and his men stood there pointing their guns, not knowing which one to shoot, as a thirty-foot-high red devil's head was lowered from the ceiling. Its mouth opened wide and a deep bass voice said, "Welcome to South Beach. Welcome to Hell." As if on cue, the glass dance floor splintered, then gave way, and squirming partygoers tumbled into the shark-filled pool.

■　■　■

The Miami morning sun shone brightly, cheerfully, mocking Fay's sadness. She wished for some gray, some overcast. Remnants of last night's sleeping pills scuba-dived in her brain as she checked the black, late-model Acura following her in the rearview mirror. She'd easily shaken the other two cars that were following her, but this bastard seemed stuck to her. So much to do, so little energy, she thought. Planning her Granny's funeral in her head, worrying about Phil. And these damn reporters, worse than no-see-ums.

She headed on 395 east toward Biscayne Bay, driving fast, faster, watching the speedometer, seventy, eighty, ninety. She hit a bump, her truck bounced, the scuba tanks in the back banging against each other, metal scraping metal. She knew she should have unloaded them.

The Acura followed her as she screeched down the expressway ramp. This asshole wasn't just another reporter, she thought, or he would have given up by now. She headed up Biscayne Boulevard, the truck trembling as she swerved onto the Venetian Causeway.

Fay saw the lights of the bridge gate, and then heard the bells of the bridge start to ring, the signal almost drowned out by the raucous strains of "Disco, Disco, Duck!" coming from a party boat, all lit up like Christmas, approaching from the south.

Granny, she thought, help me, save me. She hit the brakes instinctively and then realized that flooring it was her only chance. She stomped on the pedal. The scuba tanks, which had slid violently forward when she hit the brakes, now shot back as the truck screeched forward. When they slammed into the tailgate, they leapt up, and out into the air, in a perfect arch.

The bridgetender saw Fay's truck racing toward him on one side, the disco boat cruising toward him underneath on the other, scuba tanks flying above him, and almost directly below him, floating in the water, a big brown blob that looked like a booger.

He jammed his finger on the red stop button, and the ancient spans that had just begun to rumble upward jerked to a halt. As soon as the truck hopped over the slightly inclined span, airborne for a split second, then slamming back down on the other side with a bump and a shimmy, he threw the drawbridge lift all the way to the right, full speed, hoping it would raise up high enough to allow the disco boat under it.

But that was the least of his problems. The black Acura, apparently intent on leaping across the opening span, crashed through the blinking gate. But before it reached the center, the airborne scuba tanks crashed into the windshield at a relative velocity in excess of a hundred miles per hour.

The explosion lit up the sky behind her, but Fay just kept right on driving until she pulled into the Barnett Bank on Alton Road. She grabbed an empty grocery bag and walked into the bank. If that fisherman hadn't handed her the key in Peacock Park, she might not have

remembered this for weeks, remembered that years before, Granny had given her the duplicate key to her safe
deposit box, "just in case anything happens to me." "But
Granny," she'd protested. "Why should anything happen
to you? You're only ninety-nine."

Fay was led into the vault. She removed the box and
carried it into the cubicle and shut the door. She took a
deep breath, took out her key, took out the identical key
the fisherman had given her, and opened the box. She
couldn't believe her eyes. The box was jammed with
money, piles and piles of neatly stacked hundred-dollar
bills. Fay had never seen so much money in her life.
Resting on top of it was a sealed envelope with her
name printed neatly in her Granny's handwriting. Fay
opened it.

Dearest Fay,

> *I could not die happily as long as I knew my lover, my
> friend, my life, my bay was in danger. When the bay gave
> me the head, I realized what I had to do. I knew the head
> would be worth a lot of money to the right people. There's
> close to a million dollars in this box. Use it to save
> Biscayne Bay. But don't ask any questions about where I
> got this money. These are bad people.*

> > *I love you with all my heart,*
> > *my special Angelfish,*
> > *Granny Marion*

10

DANCE OF THE MANATEE

Vicki Hendricks

BOOGER HEARD THE crack and rumble above him as he followed the party boat upstream. He felt chills rush down his hide and each bristle on his back push against the flow. He felt his nakedness. His two-thousand-pound bulk was as vulnerable as a bowl of fish aspic.

He craved Marion, the human he called Ma. He sought the warmth of her frail flesh. But he sensed that the soft crepey arms would never again rock his fears away, nor the skeletal fingers massage the sensitive areas beneath his limbs.

She had often come to him in the moonlight when the harsh air-world was smothering her, a hot trickle of energy seeping from her pores into the salt water. He would nuzzle his rubbery nose under her armpits or into her rump till she shrieked with pleasure. They had communication beyond words. They were good for each other. Now she was gone.

His smallish brain replayed the scenario of the last afternoon he'd seen her alive. He'd been munching at the bottom, chewing well on a particularly bitter clump of turtle grass, when he'd recognized Ma's bony legs. They'd been fluttering and whipping in a foaming chaos of kicks that was sure to lure sharks. Behind her was the silent black hull of a Cigarette boat following at no-wake speed. Booger had surfaced to see Ma thrashing with her last strength through the waves, coughing, gulping air, digging in, trying to reach her Booger.

She'd led them into Booger territory, for him to save her. He felt his adrenaline-like fluids start to pump. He dove and came up in front of her. He humped her onto his rounded shoulders and made a run for the shallows, but he couldn't submerge to get up speed. Ma was gasping, and her shaking arms could barely cling around his neck.

They never had a chance. The monster boat could go most anyplace he could. It was on his tail, unstoppable as a freighter.

"Okay, Miss Marion," a male human bellowed. "No more exercise. Tell us where it is or we shoot the porker you're ridin' on."

She let go of Booger's neck instantly. He tried to nuzzle between her legs to get her back on top of him, but she was doing a scissors kick at top speed. She launched herself toward the boat. "No!" she was screaming. "No! Not him. He's innocent."

Booger ran under her and flipped and banged his tail against the boat. Once, twice. He thumped it again, again, again. It was no use. He was off balance. He got water up his nose and his lower back seized up in pain. There wasn't even a dent in the hull.

He surfaced and watched them drag Ma out of the water. There were two human males. A dark-haired, muscular one was holding Ma down. One that resembled a pale manatee was telling him what to do.

Ma lay on her stomach, flattened and exhausted, across the stern. "Head?" she panted. "That's all you want?" She snorted, coughed. "Gone. Sucker's gone."

"So where is it, Marion? Don't play senile on us," said the pale fat one.

"Ha! Sold." She wheezed. "You'll never get the money. It's hidden. It's going to a good cause."

The pointy black feet of the dark one straddled her torso, and an arm with a drawing on it grabbed a handful of her wet hair to raise her head. "We don't give a hoot about the f——ing money, ol' lady. We want the head. You're using up your time."

She turned her face up to him. "No kidding," she said. She crossed her eyes and stuck her tongue out the corner of her mouth. She giggled and snorted.

The rounded human hissed something.

Booger sensed trouble. He had to get their attention. He rolled on his side, stuck his tail at an angle, and powered. He zigged. He zagged. He did the best shark imitation he knew how.

Gold chains glinted as Pointy-foot leaned out over the water. Strong perfume drifted down and made Booger gag. "You saved that one for nothing, woman. He needs to be put out of his misery."

The pudge motioned to Pointy-foot and he let go of her hair. She looked weak and paler than ever. Booger sensed he must do something fast.

He dove to the bottom and looked, kept searching, using up the seconds. At last he found what he needed. A rock. A nice sharp piece of dead coral.

He gummed it and rose to the surface. He could hear talk, but couldn't see Ma anymore. He took the coral to the black, shiny-painted surface and dug in. He zigged. He zagged. He cut deep into the fiberglass, propelling himself the length of the boat. He gashed at the hull. He couldn't make a hole like he wanted, couldn't sink them and save Ma—no matter how hard he tried—but he cut some ridges. He would know this boat if he saw it again.

He heard Ma's voice from above. He surfaced. She was still flattened on the deck. He sensed her ebbing strength from her husky breath.

"Swim, son. Fast. Go. They have guns."

The crashing started as she spoke, and the four outboards rumbled and churned up water. Booger couldn't make it under the boat. The water was ripped again and again alongside him. He felt a zing and tasted blood, hot and frothy, in his mouth. He had to swim. He blasted away at top speed until the engines roared. He turned to catch sight of the boat skimming the water in the opposite direction.

It was sometime later he found Ma's body. He let her drift for a time, in the warm bay that she loved, but his own homing instinct made him sense he should take her near shore. She'd want her Fay-calf to know what happened.

He nudged Ma to a quiet place, where the water was less murky and the sand soft enough for them to drag her out. She was peaceful. Her lips were set in the certain way he'd noticed when she cuddled skin to hide with him in the shallows on a summer evening. She'd had the last snort on those guys.

Booger had slept and foraged, and his wounded lip stopped bleeding. He was used to pain and it was too late to worry about scarring. He watched Ma puff up till her wrinkles were gone and she resembled his true birth mother. Then the tan human brought the others to take her away.

Now as Booger listened to the sirens racing too late to the explosion on the bridge, he struggled with his grief— a feeling of outrage at the whole land-world. He relived the foul smell of perfumed male, the gold chains catching sun, the shiny black pointed feet straddling Ma's sinewy frame.

His blood began to heat. A chemical reaction took place in his disproportionate brain. The bristles on his back rose straighter, his shoulders squared, and his tail flared out and took up a steady, pulsing throb. He licked the crusty scab inside his mouth. Was it justice he wanted, or vengeance?

Whatever it was, he needed to find that marked boat.

■   ■   ■

Jake was jamming hot and heavy on his porch swing when Fay and Britt pulled into the drive. He thumped the canister on his lap in half-time with the creak of his joints. The squeak of unoiled hinges blended to produce what he thought to be an interesting rhythm.

Fay came up the steps first. "Do you think you should be flashing that head around the neighborhood, Jake?"

"Is that 'When the Saints Go Marching In'?" Britt asked. Fay snorted.

Jake stared at Britt and straightened his legs to halt the music.

"We need to take this thing to a safe place," Fay said. "Jake could be in danger."

Britt looked inside the screen door. "Never mind. His place is perfect. Anybody who comes here will figure it was already ransacked."

"That's what I like about you, Britt," Jake said.

Fay picked up the canister. "I know where you can put it—my friend Ramona's. She has snakes and iguanas. It's very secure, and she's a nurse, not a bit squeamish."

Britt put up her little finger and got Jake's attention. "What you like about me, Jake, is that I'm attractive, intelligent, kind, humorous, employed, and have female organs," she said. "I can cook too. I just don't." She punched him in the upper arm.

He grabbed his shoulder and moaned. "Damn, Britt." He moaned again. "This joint's been dislocated eight times."

"Ramona lives on the water," said Fay. "We can take the boat. It's the fastest, and maybe we'll see Booger. I feel in the mood for a swim."

"Yeah. Good idea," said Jake. A flash of Fay clad only in moonlight flickered through his brain. He'd like to take a gander at her in sunshine. She was getting even hotter with age. He massaged his joint. It was aching. "I think this is beginning to swell," he said.

"Surely you have ice," said Britt.

The women waited on the porch while Jake went inside. He took a leak, swallowed some aspirin, then grabbed a Grolsch out of the refrigerator. He rolled it over the inflamed area. Sometimes he wondered whatever had made him play football. Then he remembered—it was the money and the women.

Britt asked to use the bathroom and he directed her around cardboard boxes of briefs, then stepped back onto the porch with Fay. "You're looking lovely today," he said, and his hand reached to touch the soft tan skin of her throat.

Fay stiffened. "I've been practicing my Tae Kwon Do, Jake. When I see aggressive movement, like hands on my neck, I get nervous." She took her stance. "Ke-hap!" Her foot whipped out and stopped a half-inch from his left jaw. "I can break rocks with this."

Jake flinched. "Impressive. I was wondering if we could get together for a drink this evening. Maybe try one of those new clubs on the beach."

"I don't think so, Jake—although I'd like to see those sharks I heard about. I have too much on the brain with my Granny and all. And I'm worried sick about Phil."

There was a crash and whoosh inside the house. Britt came walking out at a fast clip. "Sorry, Jake. I touched something and started an avalanche. I hope nothing got mixed up."

Jake struggled into the back of Britt's T-Bird with the canister and popped open his beer for the short drive to Fay's boat. The traffic was heavy. They could have walked in less time. He drank the beer, and next thing he knew, Britt was slapping his cheek to wake him up.

He clomped down the dock following Fay and Britt.

"Wonder where that horny manatee is. Doesn't he usually hang out by your boat, Fay?"

"Horny?" Fay said. "Booger? Are you projecting, Jake?"

The women looked at each other. "He's so rude," Britt said. "Somebody ought to give him a well-placed kick."

Fay stepped into the boat. "Not me. It's too easy." She turned the key to start the engine, and switched on the VHF radio. Britt untied the bow line and hopped aboard.

"Jake, grab the stern and push us off, will you?" said Fay.

He handed the canister to Fay and she stowed it in the starboard locker. He unwrapped the line from the cleat and put a foot on the gunwale. The boat moved out fast, until his legs couldn't split any farther. He splashed face first into the oily bay water, got a noseful, and came up coughing. Time to cut back on the Grolsch, he thought. A plastic Winn-Dixie bag was plastered over his forehead and ear.

Fay pulled it off and put it in the bucket she had for such purposes. "Good thing you found this bag. It might have gotten wrapped around the prop." She grinned. "You need to step decisively when getting into a boat, Jake."

Jake smoothed his hair back and looked up into her green eyes. The bay paled and grayed in comparison.

"There's a ladder on the stern," she said.

"Listen to this," said Britt. She was pointing at the VHF. "There's a wounded manatee."

Fay got on the radio and requested further information. The captain came back with a description of a long jagged scar across the upper back.

"It's Booger!" said Fay. "We have to find him fast." Jake moved around toward the stern. He heard the location—north of Mattheson Hammock.

"Thanks, Captain. I'll take care of it. Let's go!" yelled Fay. She hit the throttle as Jake took the first step up the ladder. His foot slipped off the stainless-steel rung, and his 225 pounds dragged by one arm, on the side with the bad shoulder. The prop was churning a few feet from his dangling legs. He tried to yell above the engine. "Fay, stop. FAY!" he screamed. Neither she nor Britt heard.

Jake let go and fell backward, tried to yell an obscenity, but a wave choked him off. He sculled in place with one hand while he watched the boat speed away in the distance.

Jake started the short swim back to the dock. He figured he'd wait there. Fay would turn the boat around as soon as she noticed he was gone. She would feel terrible. Maybe he could convince her to go out for a drink to make up for it.

■　　■　　■

Fay headed toward Mattheson Hammock at top speed. The outlandish thought that Booger's injury had something to do with Granny's death hovered in her mind. It was more a feeling than a thought, like the sixth sense Granny had always talked about. It was beyond logic. Fay had always believed the minds of animals were badly underestimated. Someday the true potentials would be revealed, and humans would feel ashamed of their ignorant practices of slavery and butchery.

Fay slowed the boat as she neared the location. "I'll watch starboard. Britt, take port." She cut the engine to an idle and they drifted.

"Look," Britt hollered. She pointed at a half-moon shadow just visible under the edge of a dock. "There he is, just behind that black Cigarette boat." Britt blew out some air. "That's Joey G.'s dock. I don't think we should get any closer."

Fay turned to ask Jake. "Where's Jake?"

"Probably stopped off for another beer."

Fay didn't take time to ask what she meant. Booger moved out from under the dock. He raised his head. His round black eyes stared into Fay's. He did a couple slow logrolls on the surface between them and the Cigarette.

"What's the matter with him?" asked Britt.

"Must be his equilibrium is off. There's a gash in his jowl. It looks like a bullet wound, for heaven's sake."

Booger started smashing his tail flat on the surface of the water and angling his body toward the Cigarette. He smashed and angled, smashed and angled.

"I don't know what he's doing," Fay said. She pulled the boat closer and idled. "Somebody really tore up the hull of that boat. I hope they didn't kill any coral."

Booger smashed the water hard. Spray flew into the boat and drenched Britt from the shoulders down. "Damn!" she yelled. "Booger is going nuts. What's his problem?"

"I don't know, but I have a bad feeling."

Britt heard a sound and turned. Fay looked at her face and did likewise. On the dock behind them was a pudgy, balding man and a muscular, dark-haired man with a scorpion tattoo on his arm. She recognized him. "Hector," she said.

"Joey G.," said Britt, waving a hand at the fat one. "I thought you were in Fiji."

Hector lifted his other arm from his side and pointed an Uzi their way.

"Damn," said Britt. "Double damn."

"Pull your boat up to the dock, ladies," said Joey G. "We need to talk."

Fay remembered the canister in the starboard locker: big trouble. She saw the throttle out of the corner of her eye, and thought about slamming it forward. These guys were probably bluffing . . . but then she thought better. It was Miami.

She shifted into reverse to maneuver into the spot and saw Booger hide himself back under the dock. She couldn't risk Britt's life. She'd have to wing it, pick the right moment to make a move.

11

WHERE ARE YOU
DYING TONIGHT?

John Dufresne

N Biscayne Bay:

Call me Booger. Now it is November in my soul and twilight in my heart. Light is leaving me. And hope. It is this blackness above all that appalls me. The blackness to come, the blackness of this loathsome hull above me, and the inky black hearts of those Stygian scoundrels who took Ma from me, the dark-complexioned, cloven-footed desperado who fired the bullet into my snout and that pink and squabby venom spouter who steered this floating coffin. The pair of them are madness-maddened, blackness-blackened. They have all that is bloody on their minds. What lunatic vision is it that drives these blackguards? What furious passion? What unimaginable fear has freed them from the irons of civility? Loosed their bonds of horror? Nothing so simple as greed. Not that. We see differently, they and I. They have their colors, I my grays. But blackness we share. Blackness, agent of the mind, not the eye. We all see black alike. And it's blackness where our fates will meet. I have a plan.

■　　■　　■

At the Chapel of Our Lady of Perpetual Sorrow and Everlasting Anguish: Monsignor Armand Turgeon celebrated the funeral mass for his friend and patron Marion McAlister Williams. He praised her generous philanthropy, her unconventional but enthusiastic faith, her tenacious efforts to save the Everglades from the ravages of Big Sugar and the Corps of Engineers, to save the wildness that was Florida from the teeming masses breathing free, flushing waste into the bay, and paving the earth. Father Turgeon suggested that after death we return to what we were before birth—washed in the precious blood of the Lord and rocked in His mighty arms. He looked out at the assembled mourners, at the politicians, the curious, looked into the glassy eyes and disinterested faces of these waking dreamers who fend off their fears with distraction. He told them that our longing to survive is vanity only. Even God, he said, envies our mortality.

■　　■　　■

Jake Lassiter hadn't heard a word the reverend said. He'd spent the morning at the library, trying to keep his mind off Fay and Britt and where they might be and in how many pieces. He looked up "manatee" in the dictionary and learned that it comes from the Cariban *manatí*, which means breast, and for some reason he found the revelation distressing and depressing. He couldn't stop himself from thinking about that sea cow Booger, and about Fay and Britt. What kind of man beholds a hulking sausage-shaped, beaver-tailed, cleft-lipped creature and decides to name it for the female breast? A man too long at sea, perhaps. But still. Jake reminded himself where he was. He studied the Stations of the Cross on the stained-glass window. Veronica wipes the face of Jesus. He stared at the crucifix suspended above the altar, thought Jesus looked like the daring young man on the flying trapeze. Jake couldn't stop his obsessive thoughts: beaver, sausage, tail, lips, cleavage, breast. What was worse, he'd also read that a manatee's breasts were situated under the flippers, where appendage meets torso. Jake cursed himself for going to the library in the first place. It would never happen again. He turned to Janice Deal, his buddy John's ex, smiled, squeezed her hand. She smiled, returned her attention to the priest. Jake inhaled her vanilla scent. He tried not to think of breasts in her armpits.

■　■　■

Judge Manuel Dominguez wondered why this priest was carrying on about the failure of a people to cast off its oppressors. Quebec, he was yapping about, not Cuba. Not a very apt or decorous sermon, certainly. What did all this have to do with the death of this esteemed grande dame?

Had he missed something? All this sadness. First his nephew Victor and now Ms. Williams. Poor Victor, a lousy bailiff, sure, and a worse jai alai player. "Victorless" they called him at the fronton. But why would he try to do that, race the drawbridge like he did in the new Acura? With the young, the judge thought, often the danger is in not taking the risk.

∎ ∎ ∎

Vernon Sawyer wanted to sing "What Wondrous Love Is This?" "Abide with Me," or "There Is Power in the Blood," anything. Why can't Catholics sing? He was tired with all this talk, talk, talk. He wanted his religion to carry him out of the church, out of himself, to lift his heart, to set his feet in ecstasy. He looked at the hair of this vaguely familiar man seated in front of him, saw how it thinned at the crown. He hated the treachery of baldness. Vernon knew that when there is a mystery, there are always two stories—what happened and what seemed to happen. What seemed to happen here was a drowning. But no, not with the granddaughter gone missing like she'd done. That was no coincidence, no sir. Something to do with that key he'd passed to Fay. The key to the whole mystery, likely.

∎ ∎ ∎

Dash Brandon didn't like his seat. He belonged up there with Governor What's-his-face and Jimmy Carter. This sort of affront would never happen at Planet Hollywood or at the Raleigh, where just this morning he'd been seated by Johnnie Cochran's table. What was he in town for? Defending some fat tourist? Something about a riot. Or was it the Club Hell fiasco? Dash had given Johnnie a nod and a conspiratorial thumbs-up. He'd eavesdropped as Johnnie rehearsed his forensic couplets: "If the facts don't indicate, you must vindicate," "If the fault's with the police, you must release," and so on throughout the brunch. Dash thought about his own funeral. A full-couch, polished copper casket with taffeta lining, interior lighting, brass fittings. Or an Egyptian sarcophagus. Wouldn't that be a hoot? Show tunes and spontaneous eulogies. He cast his pallbearers: Arnold, Bruce, Sly, Wesley, Woody, the Boz. No, not the Boz. Denzel. Ziff Bodine nudged Dash, showed him the sketch he'd been doodling. Castro, it looked like, without the beard and toupee.

■   ■   ■

John Deal wondered if this was such a good idea, coming back to Miami. It had seemed like the right thing, sitting there in the bar with Mike, into his tenth Cuba libre, thinking he could straighten his whole life out in a minute if he could just get back home. He felt an intense heat at the base of his neck, an itch on his scalp that stung like shame. He touched the back of his head. He made a mental note: call 1-800-ROGAINE. Why the burn? Why at the back of his head. Too much Advil? Where was it coming from? Deal turned, and the man's doleful gaze locked with his for a moment. Deal returned his eyes to the altar. Where had he seen that face before? Havana? Not Havana. Deal felt—he didn't know—he was marked or something. That's it. The Grove. The man outside the market. Just a coincidence, he hoped. What was it his dad used to say? You'll meet everyone twice before you die. This was like a reunion for Deal. The man behind him, his ex across the aisle with Jake Lassiter of all people, the movie actor who'd sued him over the hot tub. Deal wondered if he might be dreaming all this. No, this was Mike Weston right beside him, Mike Weston was real, wasn't he? And there's that quack, Irwin Schein . . . berg? man? Schein? . . .

■   ■   ■

Irwin Scheinblum wondered why the cover-up. Marion's death was no drowning, of course. You don't have to be a coroner to know that it takes days for a drowned body to bloat with gas and rise to the surface. No weeds or sand in the lungs. He'd read the autopsy report. Evidence of petechiae, tiny hemorrhages, dark spots on the mucous membrane, caused most likely by increased pressure in the head from strangling, or choking perhaps. Face and neck congested and dark red, bruises on the arms and legs, contusions on the face, a fractured hyoid bone and torn thyroid cartilage. So why did the medical examiner rule the death an accident? And why wasn't anyone upset? Why wasn't anyone talking, writing about this? Irwin was puzzled. Irwin needed several drinks.

∎ ∎ ∎

Marion McAlister Williams felt deflated, degenerate, annoyed. So there you have it: there are no answers beyond the grave. Well, not the grave just yet. No answers beyond death. She was no longer one of the chosen people— those still alive. She found herself humming the tune to "The Yellow Rose of Texas" and singing the words to Emily Dickinson poems: Because I could not stop for death, *da-da-da-dum-dee-tum*. No answers and no tunnels and no lights. We spend our lives lumbering from hope to hope. So what is death then? No lights and no hope. Marion felt like her mind was going blind. Death belongs to life, not to whatever-this-is. No hope and no Buddha. No Jesus. No Allah. No angels, no time, no enlightenment, no nine circles of hell, no rest, no numbers, no regrets, no color, no stories, no space, no peace, no honor, no pain, no blood, no air, no matter. Just alone. All alone. That's all.

∎ ∎ ∎

Jimmy Carter was basking in a marvelous run of good luck and nothing was going to get him down—not Rosalynn's volatile mood swings, not Robertico Robles's threats, not this dismal ceremony, and certainly not these elitist book reviewers. Jimmy Carter stood with the congregation. He bent his head, moved his lips, as if in prayer. Yesterday he'd autographed eight hundred hardcover copies of *Always a Reckoning* in two hours at Books and Books, beating the Anne Rice record by seventy-five books. Mitchell Kaplan told him so, and booksellers don't lie. And then last night he'd beaten Vanilla Ice by a pentameter in the poetry slam at Warehaus 57. Then this morning's *News* carried his photo on page one. There he was driving a nail into a crossbeam in the new Habitat house in Liberty City. He was in a zone right now, and he dared to dream of, to lust in his heart for, the unprecedented Double Nobel— Peace and Literature. He was possessed by the Muse, on fire with a Promethean mission to steal poetry from the academic gods and deliver it to the people. Soon poetry would be accessible to working men and women in paper-hat jobs, would be understood and loved by schoolchildren, illiterates, babies, cats. And in the limo on the way to the cemetery he'd begin his *Sonnet Sequence for Democracy*, that is, if he could get Governor Whatchamacallit to shut his trap for a minute.

■   ■   ■

Former altar boy Juan Carlos Reyes stood in line to receive Communion. *Introibo ad altare Dei.* The choir chanted *Tantum Ergo.* To God the joy of my youth. He felt his pager vibrate in his pocket. He checked the display. Ramona calling. Probably wanted him to pick up a bag of those pink mice for her snakes. I have no shame, he thought. Shame is for the young. Juan Carlos nodded to the Peanut Man as he passed the first pew. We live on secrets, he thought. He took the host in his hands. My God, what would the world be like if all our secrets were revealed, all our lusts, opinions, fears, dreams, our fantasies, our rituals? What secrets, he wondered, did this old woman take with her? Expensive secrets perhaps. Well, he wasn't here to worry about that. He was here to protect his holdings: Reyes Cuban-American Cruise Lines, Reyes Hotel and Casinos, Reyes PepsiCo Bottling Company, Reyes Burger King Havana, Inc. He was here to keep his eye on the slippery Dr. Irwin Scheinblum, the one man alive who could positively identify the body of Fidel Castro, the man who had performed Fidel's penile implant in 1962. But where was that body? Juan Carlos was not paying a million dollars to any *Cuban* Cuban for a severed head. The gentleman would have to provide the rest of the filthy Communist. Of course, if he, himself, could acquire the rumored lock of hair and match its DNA with the head, well, perhaps then he would negotiate. Yes, people will need to be relocated. Yes, people will have to die, unfortunately. Yes, of course, the transition to the Golden Age of freedom and prosperity will not be easy.

■   ■   ■

This was still not what Joe Sereno had in mind when he joined the police department. This was not fighting crime; this was not making a difference. This was standing in the vestibule of a church waiting for some dignitaries to exit to their limousines. He'd been reduced to this, to special-detail security for Magic City Protective Services. He'd been suspended without pay after the Grove riot and would remain suspended until the trial was over, at least. And now he had to worry if Johnnie Cochran was going to turn him into the next Mark Fuhrman. Sure he'd called the fat guy a Canuck and a Frog, but he hadn't meant it in a bad way. Since when did people start worrying about the Frenchies, anyway? And now he was getting that uneasy feeling again like on the night of the Club Hell disaster when he worked the door. Who'd have thought the sharks would only go after the lawyers like they did? Must be some kind of pheromone they give off. What a mess that was. Joe Sereno himself had dragged two of the bodies out of the drink—the city manager of Miami Beach, who looked like a drowned cat, actually, and the city's insurance attorney, Russell B. Whittaker III, whose mascara had run over his face and whose left arm had been chewed to the bone. Joe felt dizzy again. Maybe he was bad luck like the sergeant said. He dipped his fingers into the holy water font, blessed himself. He waited for whatever would happen to happen.

■   ■   ■

In Dania: When housewife Sabrina Kennedy saw the face of Mickey Schwartz on the door of her Kelvinator refrigerator, saw it blossom to life like a Polaroid photograph, why, she called Tristan Jude, Dania correspondent for the *Broward Sun-Tattler* and invited him over to see for himself. He wanted to know what she thought this meant. Well, she said, it means, apparently, that I'm going to win the lottery in the very near future. Yes, she had to agree with Tristan, this could possibly be Mickey's double, that Cuban dude, in which case she figured she'd meet some tall, dark stranger. Miracles aren't ordinary, she told him. Life's no accident. Everything means something.

■ ■ ■

On Desi Arnaz Boulevard: Big Joey G. leaned against the fireplace, his arm resting on the onyx mantel, in his hand a Vietnamese trophy skull. "We boiled the flesh off the VC skulls," he told Britt. "We made table ornaments, ashtrays, candy dishes, like this fellow here. I call him Tranh. Sometimes we carved their ulnas into letter openers, their fingers into whistles." He set the skull on the mantel, sat in the club chair across from Britt. "Happiest days of my life, the war."

"And now you find yourself playing with skulls again," Britt said. "How funny."

"Not playing, Ms. Montero. Neurosuspension is not a game." Big Joey explained the process: A cryonicist opens the subject's chest, injects cryopreservatives and cooling solutions through the blood vessels to preserve the brain. He then severs the head at the sixth cervical vertebra, submerges the skull in a silicone oil bath with dry ice for twenty-four hours. "Then we pop the noodle in a neurocan and cool it in liquid nitrogen for ten days."

Britt stretched her shackled legs on the couch. "Why just the head? Why not the whole body? Why not a corpsicle?"

"Cephalic isolation is economical, portable. The body isn't very useful really."

"Speak for yourself."

"Eventually, we bring back the cryonaut, and he's himself, only we make him better because we provide an engineered body, a cyborg, a person who can breathe underwater or run like the wind."

"Fidel the flying squirrel, maybe?"

Big Joey smiled.

"You can't make a flank steak back into a cow, Big Joey. The thermally challenged will remain so."

The doorbell chimed. Big Joey G. stood, excused himself. "That would be our delivery: Lilia Sands and her faux Fidel."

Britt said, "This is getting confusing."

∎　　∎　　∎

On the patio, Hector explained to Fay how it was, but how could a woman ever understand? "Yes, I killed your grandmother. Yes, I killed Phil. What were we supposed to do when he let you escape like he did? You think I had a choice? Besides, he was a nudge and you know it."

Fay wiped her tears on her shoulder. "Scum!" She knew she'd destroy Hector if she could chew her way through these cuffs and the ropes.

"I understand you're upset, but don't you see that the crime itself is a relief, you know, a release. It's a regeneration." Hector stood and stretched. He kissed his scorpion tattoo, flicked his tongue at Fay. He thought, Yes, this woman will understand. "Before I killed, I was far more horrible than I am now, because I was pregnant with evil, with the idea of murder. And now the evil is done, gone, vanished. The idea of violence, the threat of violence, is always more frightening than the act of violence. Don't you think?'' Fay heard a chime, a tune that sounded like "Lara's Theme" from *Dr. Zhivago.*

"Our guests have arrived," Hector said. "And now we're all going for a long boat ride.''

■   ■   ■

At the Odyssey Motel: Fidel Castro sat on his balcony smoking his Don Miguel de la Flor cigar, watching the topless bathers on the beach. Oxen in the sun, he thought. Fidel winced, lifted his weight off the chair as a shock of pain shot through his groin. What more, he wondered, can this hulk suffer? He'd done the surgery, the radiation, had the orchiectomy. Too late. The cancer had spread to the lymph nodes and the bone and to distant organs. Nothing left now but hormones and morphine. There he sat, anonymous in his morbidity, hairless and shrunken, listening to a Xavier Cugat CD in the heart of the city that wanted his head at any price. Drawn here, made reckless, by love.

Fidel took the photo of Lilia Sands out of his shirt pocket. Oh, there had been others—Miss This, Miss That, Miss The Other. They were all lovely, but like flowers without scent compared to Lilia. She was his first socialist. I kiss the feet of you, señorita, he told her that night in his tent in the Sierra Maestra. He closed his eyes, tried to summon Lilia, his Penelope. Yes, he thought, yes, because she never did a thing like that before as bite my ear—her breakfast in bed—never a thing as cut a lock of my hair. Lilia, her boiled eyes and smutty photos, her samba, her wicked tongue. I gave her all the pleasure I could until she said yes and yes. I let her see my everything. O Lilia! O Cuba! My twin lovers! Yes, I know the back alleys of my heart, the dark corners of my soul, and though I tried to do you no harm, in the trying I failed. Love without commitment, socialism without democracy are doomed. Yes, I was seduced by revolution, driven to trample the worm who sold our country to the Mafia and the corporations, to trample him and drag his carcass ten times around the gates of Havana. A new order, I thought. A New Jerusalem. But politics is just who shoves whom, who doles out the pineapples and soup to whom, who pockets whose profits. Politics is a marketing strategy, a tool of business. It can never make anyone happy. For that we need virtue and knowledge, not laws.

And so I get to live my simple life at last, here in the land of the lotus-eaters, where our people, some of them, have lost the hope of home. Others are worms who would devour our flesh. The aristocrats who fled, the professional class. I wouldn't give a snap of my fingers for all their learning, their fortunes, their self-righteousness. Let them try to create something, like an independent nation, like a poem. Yes, when at last this Cuban-head-as-Trojan-horse business sorts itself out, the exiles will be coming home. To those who return, welcome, but remember, no one will own us—the *Cuban* Cubans, we who have lived on our wandering rock for the last thirty-seven years. You see, we know how you think: eleven million Cubans—Demon Nation; one billion Chinese—Most Favored Nation. We understand the great fear in your adopted country, the USA: fear of the poor! Power is based on weakness of the masses. Those who come home must serve the people, not judge them, command them, prod them. Cubans, yes. Juan Carlos Reyes, no, no *gusanos,* no problem.

Fidel thought again of Lilia, her legs and her lips. He remembered the moon setting over the Gulf of Manzanillo, his comrade Che, and his heart was going like mad. Yes, Lilia, he said, señorita, yes, I will, yes and yes.

12

THE ODYSSEY

Elmore Leonard

**J**OE S<small>ERENO</small> <small>CAUGHT</small>
the Odyssey night clerk as he was going off: prissy guy,
had his lunch box under his arm.

"I saw it this morning on TV," Joe said. "So there was a
lot of excitement, huh? I thought the cops'd still be here,
at least the crime scene guys. I guess they've all cleared
out. You hear the shots? You must've."

"I was in the office," the night guy said.

Joe wondered how this twink knew he was in the office
at the exact time the shots were fired. What'd he think, it
was soundproof in there? But the cops no doubt had
asked him that, so Joe let it pass and said, "It was the two
guys in one-oh-five, wasn't it?"

"I think so."

"You're not sure?"

The night guy rolled his eyes and then pretended to yawn. He did things like that, had different poses.

"Fairly respectable-looking guys," Joe said, "but no luggage. What're they doing, shacking up? Maybe, maybe not. But I remember thinking at the time, they're up to something. The TV news didn't mention their names, so there must not've been any ID on the bodies and the cops didn't think the names they used to register were really theirs. Am I right?"

The night guy said, "I wouldn't know," acting bored.

"Soon as I saw those guys yesterday—they checked in as I was getting ready to go off—I said to Mel, 'Let me see the registration cards, see what names they gave.' He wouldn't show me. He goes, 'Registering guests is not a security matter, if you don't mind.'" Mel, the day guy, sounding a lot like Kenneth, the night guy.

"I didn't have time to hang around, keep an eye on them," Joe went on. "I had to go to another job, a function at the Biltmore. They put on extra security for this bunch of Cuban hotshots meeting there. I mean *Cuban* Cubans, said to be Castro sympathizers, and there was a rumor Fidel himself was gonna show up. You believe it? I wore a suit instead of this Mickey Mouse uniform, brown and friggin' orange; I get home I can't wait to take it off. Those functions, you stand like this holding your hands in front of you, like you're protecting yourself from getting a hernia, and you keep your eyes moving. So"—he gestured toward the entrance—"I saw the truck out there, the tan van, no writing on the sides? That's the cleanup company, right?''

"I wouldn't know," the night guy said.

Little curly-haired twink, walked with his knees together.

"Well, listen, I'll let you go," Joe said, "and thanks for sharing that information with me, it was interesting. I'll go check on the cleanup people, see how they're doing. What room was that again, one-oh-five?''

■   ■   ■

It sure was.

There was furniture in the hall by the open door and a nasty smell in the air. As Joe approached, a big black guy in a white plastic jumpsuit, latex gloves, what looked like a shower cap, goggles up on his head, blue plastic covering his shoes, came out carrying a floor lamp.

Joe said, "Joe Sereno, security officer."

"I'm Franklin, with Baneful Clean-Up."

"*Bane*ful?''

"The boss named it. He tried Pernicious Clean-Up in the Yellow Pages? Didn't get any calls."

Joe said, "Hmmmm, how about Death Squad?"

"That's catchy," Franklin said, "but people might get the wrong idea. You know, that we doing the job 'stead of cleaning up after. This is my partner, Marlis," Franklin said, and Joe turned to see a cute young black woman approaching in her plastic coveralls, hip-hop coming out of the jam box she was carrying.

"Joe Sereno, security officer."

"Serene, yeah," Marlis said, "that's a cool name, Joe," her body doing subtle, funky things like it was plugged into the beat. She said to Franklin, "Diggable Planets doing 'Rebirth of Slick.' 'It's cool like dat.' "

" 'It's chill like dat,' " Franklin said. "Yeah, 'it's chill like dat.' "

Franklin bopping now, going back into the room.

Joe followed him in, stopped dead at the sight, and said, "Oh, my God," at the spectacle of blood: on the carpet, on two walls, part of the ceiling, a trail of blood going from this room into the bathroom. Joe looked in there and said it again, with feeling, "Oh, my God."

"Like they was skinnin' game in here," Franklin said. "Shotgun done one of them at close range. The other one, nine-millimeter pistol, they believe. Man got shot four times through and through—see the holes in the wall there? They dug out the bullets. Made it to the bathroom, got three more pumped into him and bled out in the shower. Thank you, Jesus. We still have to clean it, though, with the green stuff, get in between the tiles with a toothbrush. We thankful the man came in here, didn't go flop on the bed to expire."

Joe said, "Man, the smell."

"Yeah, it's what your insides get like exposed to the air too long, you know what I'm saying? Your viscera, it's called. It ain't too bad yet. But if you gonna stay in here and watch," Franklin said, "better breathe through your mouth."

Joe said, "I think I'll step out to the patio for a minute."

■   ■   ■

The two secretaries from Dayton, Ohio, their bra straps hanging loose, were out by the pool already, this early in the morning, to catch some rays, working at it, not wasting a minute of their vacation. Joe took a few deep breaths, inhaling the morning air to get that smell out of his nose. On the other side of the pool, still in shade, a guy sat in a plastic patio chair smoking a cigar as he watched the girls. Guy in his sixties—he'd be tall with a heavy frame; his body hadn't seen much sun, but his face was weathered. Joe believed the guy was wearing a rug. Black hair that had belonged to a Korean woman at one time. A retired wigmaker had told him they used a lot of Korean hair. This one looked too dark for a guy in his sixties. Joe had never noticed the guy before—he must've checked in yesterday or last night—but for some reason he looked familiar. Joe went back in the unit, ducked into the bedroom and picked up the phone.

"Sereno, security. Who's in one-twenty?"

The day guy's voice said, "Why do you want to know?"

I'm doing something wrong, Joe thought. I'm failing to communicate. "Listen, it's important. The guy, there's something about him isn't right."

"Like what?"

"I think he's using the Odyssey as a hideout."

"Is this the guy with the Steven Seagal hairpiece?"

"You got it."

"Just a minute."

The twink was gone at least five minutes while Joe

waited, trying to breathe through his mouth. Finally he came back on.

"His name's Garcia."

∎ ∎ ∎

Franklin was working on the ceiling with a sponge mop; he would come down off his metal ladder and squeeze into a pail, then take the pail into the bathroom and dump it in the toilet. Marlis was scrubbing a wall with what looked like a big scouring pad, moving in time to the beat coming from the jam box, kind of spastic, Joe thought, but sexy all the same.

The two looked like they were dressed up in moon suits they'd made for Halloween: the white plastic coveralls, goggles, respiratory masks, covered head to toe. The smell of the chemicals they were using was even stronger now than the other smell. Joe got a whiff and started coughing as he asked Marlis what it was they cleaned with.

She said, "The green stuff for a lot of heavy, dried blood; the pink stuff when it isn't too old and hard to get off."

"Girl," Franklin said, "your head keeps touching the wall and I see some hair sticking out."

"I'll fix it in a minute."

Marlis had on rubber gloves that came up her arms. She said to Joe Sereno, "See these little specks here in the wall? They from the man's skull, little tiny fragments of bone. Sometime I have to use pliers to pull them out. This dark stuff is the dude's hair. See these other holes? They from the shotgun." She funked around, doing steps to the music as she said to Franklin, "Coolio, for your pleasure."

Franklin listened and said, "Ain't Coolio." Listened some more, said, "You got your Cools confused. It's LL Cool J, no other, 'cause that's 'Hey Lover.' " He paused, looking past Marlis to a framed print on the wall. "Girl, is that like modern art on there or something else?"

Marlis went up to the picture for a close look and said, "It's something else."

Joe looked at it and said, "Oh, my God."

He watched Marlis remove the print and drop it into a red bag. "Ain't worth cleaning. Anything has body fluids, tissue, poo-poo, you know, anything biohazardous, goes in these bags. We give them to a company takes care of medical waste to get rid of."

"You missed a speck there," Franklin said, pointing at the wall.

"I'm still working on it, baby." Lowering her voice, she said to Joe, "He don't like to see me talking to other men."

"Are you and him married?"

"You'd think so to hear him."

"I was wondering, is there any money in cleanup work? You don't mind my asking."

"We quoted this job at fifteen hundred. Hey, how many people can you find to do it? Another reason it's a good business, recessions don't bother it none. This one here looks worse'n it is. Doesn't smell too bad. You work where a body's been decomposing awhile, now you talking about smell. Like old roadkill up close? You go home and take a shower, you have to wash out your nostrils good. The smell like sticks to the hairs in your nose.''

"What's the worst one you ever had to clean up?''

"The worst one. Hmmmm.'' She said, "You mean the very worst one? Like an advanced state of decomp has set in? The body's in a dark, damp place and dung beetles have found it?''

Franklin said, "Girl?''

"I'm coming,'' Marlis said. She got a scraper, like a big putty knife, from a box of tools and went back to work. She said to Joe, "It dries on here it's hard to get off.''

"What is that?''

She was scraping at something crusted on there. "Little piece of what the dude used to use to think with. His brain, honey. He maybe should've thought better about coming here, huh? Two dudes die and nobody even knows who they are. Least it's what I heard.'' She looked over at Joe Sereno standing by the closet door, staring at the knob. "Don't touch that, baby.''

"It looks like candle wax,'' Joe said, "but I don't see any candles in the room.''

"It ain't wax,'' Marlis said, "it's some more the dude's gray matter. Gets waxy like that outside the head. See how the wood's splintered right above it? That's from skull fragments shot in there. This one dude, I swear, is all over the room.''

"You just do murders?''

"Homicides, suicides, and decompositions.''

"How about animals?''

"Once in a while. We cleaned up after a woman

poisoned her dogs, fifteen of 'em she couldn't feed no more. It smelled worse'n a dead manatee laying in the sun too long."

Joe perked up. "There's a manatee over on the bay was shot. You hear about it?"

Joe thought he saw a look pass between Marlis and Franklin on the ladder as she said no, she didn't think so. "A pretty friendly creature," Joe said, "used to play with that old woman who was killed. Marion something?"

"McAlister Williams," Marlis said. "Yeah, I've heard of her. Hundred and two years old and still swimmin' in the bay."

Joe said, "And there was that guy tried to jump the drawbridge and didn't make it."

"Name was Victor," Franklin said, down from the ladder, heading for the john with his pail. "Actually was a scuba tank I understand flew out of a truck, hit the man's car and blew him up. Totaled 'em both. Yeah, we heard about that. 'Cool like dat.' " He said, "So-Lo Jam," and right away said, "I take that back."

"You better," Marlis said.

"That's from *Cold Chillin'*, so it has to be Kool G. Rap. Yeah."

Joe had to wait, not having any idea what they were talking about, before saying, "How about that disaster at Club Hell? I was working there that night. It was horrible."

"Nobody had to clean that one up," Franklin said, coming out of the john, "the sharks took care of it."

"Come here for a minute, will you?" Joe motioned them over to the sliding glass door that led to the patio.

"See that guy sitting by the pool? Over on the other side. Who does he look like?"

"I can't see him good," Franklin said.

"Take your goggles off."

Franklin squinted now, eyes uncovered. He said, "I don't know. Who?"

Marlis came over and right away said, "The dude with the cigar? He looks like Castro. Either Castro or that dude goes around thinking he looks like Castro. You know what I'm saying? Mickey Something-or-other's his name. Yeah, Mickey Schwartz."

"Wait a minute," Franklin said, still squinting. "What Castro you talking about?"

"Castro, the one from Cuba."

"They *all* from Cuba."

"What's his name—Fidel," Marlis said. "Fidel Castro. Shaved off his beard." She paused and hunched in a little closer to Joe and Franklin. "Shaved his beard and must've shaved his head, too, 'cause the man's wearing a rug."

"That's what I thought too," Joe said. "But whose hair does the rug look like?"

Now Marlis squinted till she had it and said, "Yeah, that high-waisted cat kung-fus everybody he don't shoot."

Franklin said, "I know who you mean. That kung-fu cat with the big butt. Doesn't take shuck and jive from nobody. But listen to me now. If that's *the* Fidel we talking about here, there's a man will pay a million dollars to see him dead. Man name of Reyes. It would be easy as pie to cap him sitting there, wouldn't it?" He looked at Joe Sereno. "I mean if it was your trade."

"Tempting," Marlis said, "but safer to clean up after. Celebrity, be nothing wrong with doubling the fee."

Joe was thinking. He said, "You suppose a hit man killed these two in here?"

"Hit men as a rule," Franklin said, "don't make this kind of mess. One on the back of the head, use a twenty-two High Standard Field King with a suppressor on it. We've followed up after hit men, haven't we, precious?"

"We sure have," Marlis said. "Lot of that kind of work around here."

Joe Sereno said, "You don't suppose . . ." and stopped, narrowing his eyes then to make what he wanted to say come out right. "In the past few days I've run into three homicides, counting these two, and a fourth one they're calling an accident looks more like a homicide to me. I have a hunch they're related. Don't pin me down for the motive, 'cause I don't see a nexus. At least not yet I don't. But I got a creepy feeling that once these two are identified, it will explain the others. I'm talking about the old woman, and a guy named Phil. And, unless I miss my guess, it all has something to do with that man sitting over there smoking a cigar."

"Unless," Marlis said, "the dude over there is the Fidel impersonator, Mickey Schwartz."

"Either way," Joe Sereno said, "ID these two and this whole mess will become clear."

A look passed between Franklin and Marlis.

Joe caught it and thought, Hmmmm.

THE LAW

OF THE JUNGLE

Carl Hiaasen

ICKEY SCHWARTZ HAD never been to Bimini, as there was not among Bahamians a huge demand for Fidel Castro impersonators.

Nor had Mickey Schwartz ever been in a Cigarette boat crossing the Gulf Stream with an Uzi-toting goon, an obese fugitive politician, two crabby female hostages, and an older woman who elegantly claimed to have slept with the real Fidel.

In that respect, it was the most interesting gig of Mickey Schwartz's show business career. And, except for the threat of gunplay, it was also the most gratifying, professionally.

Being a Castro impersonator in Miami was no picnic—a

vast impassioned segment of the population regarded the Cuban leader more as a murderous butcher than as cheap comic relief. As Mickey Schwartz could attest, there was no fortune to be made milking Castro for laughs, at least not in South Florida.

Most of Mickey's Fidel gigs were weekend parades in Little Havana, and involved long hours of pretending to be dead—lying in an open casket, swinging from a gallows, rotting under a cloud of fake flies in a cane field . . . that sort of thing. As long as Mickey didn't move a muscle, everything was fine; people cheered like crazy.

Easy payday, his pals would say. But Mickey Schwartz hated it. The fatigues were stifling and the phony beard was scratchy. Besides, he was too talented for Sunday parade crap. He had a solid lounge act in Sunny Isles—Brando, Nicholson, Robin Williams. He even did a Howard Stern, for the younger crowd. Who else did a Howard Stern? Nobody, that's who.

Mickey Schwartz believed he hated impersonating Castro nearly as much as the exiles hated Castro himself. Yet now, plowing across the Gulf Stream in a spiffy black Cigarette boat, he figured all the hard humiliating work was paying off. Ten grand, and a free trip to Bimini!

Mickey wasn't sure exactly who was paying him, and didn't care. He was feeling pretty good about the day, until the speedboat hit the curling wake of an oil tanker and the humongous fugitive politician—the one they called Big Joey G.—choked to death on his conch salad.

■　■　■

Fay Leonard said, "Tell me you're not just throwing him overboard."

Hector squinted at her. "No, baby, I'm not throwing him overboard. I'm rolling him overboard."

The body of Big Joey disappeared over the transom. The splash was majestic. Fay glared at Hector; she hated polluters.

Hector said, "That oughta add about eight knots to our cruising speed."

"And three hundred pounds of filth to the water column," Fay muttered.

"No, baby, that man is definitely biodegrading."

Britt Montero, shackled on the deck next to Fay, couldn't help but snigger. Hector winked and flexed, making the scorpion tattoo do a shimmy. He slipped the strap of the Uzi over his shoulder and returned to the wheel. Fay's gaze shifted to the red Gott cooler at Hector's feet. Glumly she considered what was inside, packed on a pillow of ice.

Nothing left to bargain with now, she thought. The granddaughter of Marion McAlister Williams will soon be sleeping with the fishes, and Joey G.

Fay felt an elbow in her ribs. Britt leaned close and said, "Don't worry." Fay nodded gamely. Maybe they could talk their way out of it. Maybe there was hope.

Just as the despicable Hector had predicted, the newly lightened Cigarette boat picked up speed. In her mind,

Fay replayed the long ride. By the time Joey G. started gagging, everyone aboard had grown sick of him. His preposterous cryogenics spiel had become a topic of open ridicule among the captives; even Hector admitted it was baloney, along with the Vietnam skull-boiling rap. Nobody who saw Big Joey cram an entire quart of diced conch into his voluminous cheeks could've imagined him as a soldier in any man's army, in any war.

Then came the jolt of the tanker wake, a shower of salt spray, and Joey was flopping on the deck like an albino walrus. Hector flung himself across the Gott cooler to prevent it from being kicked overboard. Before the others realized Big Joey wasn't reenacting some ludicrous jungle-sapper fantasy, it was over. All of Hector's strength was required to jettison the prebloated corpse.

At the splash, the elegant older Cuban woman made a sign of the cross. Her escort, the guy dressed up to look like Castro, blurted: "Doesn't anybody here know the Heimlich?"

"Oh yeah. The Heimlich." Hector peered over the transom. "Gee, I guess it's too late."

He cranked the outrageous four Mercs and set a course for the Bimini islands. "Bastard," hissed Fay Leonard, but her words were lost in the high roar of the big outboards.

■　　■　　■

Booger the manatee had watched from a depth of nine feet as the black speedboat idled from the slender channel into Biscayne Bay. He didn't know the boat was headed for the ocean, then the Bahamas. He didn't know who was on board, or why. He didn't know the dark purpose of the voyage.

In fact there was much Booger didn't know, wouldn't know, couldn't know, since his brain was approximately the size and complexity of a bocci ball. Booger's breadth of rumination was therefore limited to a daily quest for warm quiet waters, tasty seaweed, and (once in a great while) clumsy sea cow sex.

Whatever had gotten into this manatee in recent days coursed like a mysterious fever, temporarily investing him with the cunning of a dolphin, the fierce agility of a killer whale, and the dopey loyalty of a Labrador retriever. None of those qualities typically was found in *Trichechus manatus*—an ancient, migratory, dull, but delightfully docile hulk of mammal.

The death of the old woman, for example, had stirred in Booger the utterly alien feelings of sorrow, rage, a thirst for revenge. No mere manatee was ever burdened by such complicated emotions! For most, bliss was never farther than the next juicy clump of turtle grass.

In a way, Booger's gunshot wound was a blessing. Eventually the nagging sting in his flank chased away the brain fever and unclouded his primordial thinking.

Lolling under the dock at Big Joey's house, Booger found himself losing the insane urge to chase boats, slap his tail on the surface like some hyperthyroid beaver, or attach strange names ("Ma"—what the heck did that mean?) to pale wrinkled humans.

As daylight slipped away, Booger was cogitating less like a Disney character and more like an ordinary sea cow. He no longer fretted over what was happening in the bright dry world above him. Likewise, the fate of other species was no longer Booger's worry—a kitten could either swim, or it couldn't. And presented with a choice between rescuing a drowning person and dodging the propellers of a lunatic Donzi, Booger wouldn't hesitate to dive for cover.

Sorry, pal. Every mammal for himself.

As darkness fell, Booger swam slowly into the bay. He kept to the shoreline and meandered north toward the familiar bustle of Dinner Key. When he got there, he was startled to find swimming among the sailboats another manatee, shy and sleek and miraculously unscarred. As she brushed against him, Booger felt a tingle in his fluke.

Soon the bullet wound was forgotten, as were the queer events of recent days and the fading clamor of Coconut Grove. Together the two sea cows struck out across the silky waters, breaching and diving in tandem. Booger knew of a little out-of-the-way place on Virginia Key, a quiet teardrop of a harbor where friendly human shrimpers occasionally tossed crispy heads of lettuce to visiting manatees.

It was a helluva first date.

■　■　■

The yacht of Juan Carlos Reyes was anchored in a gentle chop a mile east of North Bimini. Even for Hector it was easy to find: a gleaming 107-foot Feadship called *Entrante Presidente*.

Reyes greeted them in a navy blazer, cream-colored slacks, and dainty Italian loafers. The yacht's salon reeked of cigars and heavy cologne. Britt and Fay instantly became sick. Reyes ordered them taken to a private cabin and handcuffed to a bedpost. Hector eagerly volunteered, but Reyes told him to sit down. One of Reyes's bodyguards, a weightlifter type with a pearl nose stud, escorted the women away.

Juan Carlos appraised the Castro impersonator. "The real one was heavier in the belly," he said, circling, "but overall, my friend, you're not bad."

"Thank you," said Mickey Schwartz. He had a routine to go with the getup: a bombastic and humorously convoluted tirade against Yankee imperialists, capitalism, and blue jeans.

Juan Carlos Reyes wasn't interested in hearing it. "You must be Lilia," he said to the elegant older woman. He attempted to kiss her hand, but she pulled it away.

"Little fool," she scoffed. "Cuba will never take you back."

"We shall see, *puta.*"

Lilia bent over (for she was a full six inches taller than Juan Carlos Reyes) and slapped him smartly on the face, dislodging the smoldering nub of his cigar. Hector sprang forward, raising the stubby Uzi, but Reyes waved him off.

"Fidel is ten times the man you'll ever be," said Lilia Sands.

Reyes smiled. "Your precious Fidel is dead, old woman. Croaked. Cacked. Deceased. Checked out. Whacked. Eighty-sixed. *Muerto.* Your *amor* is no more."

With frost in her voice, Lilia declared, "I do not believe you, *enanillo!*"

"Ah, but my sources are impeccable." Juan Carlos

Reyes plucked the cigar off the carpet and relit it. "The highest of connections in Washington—and yes, Havana." He turned to Hector. "Do you have it?"

Hector nodded, fished in a pocket. He brought out a wispy lock of dark hair, tied in a red and gold Montecristo wrapper. He handed it to Reyes, who examined it as if it were a rare jewel.

"In a cigar box," Hector said, "in her bedroom."

Reyes chuckled. "Ironic, no?"

Lilia glared defiantly. Mickey Schwartz deduced it was not the appropriate moment to mention his fee. He stared down at his black military boots, crusty with salt from the boat ride.

Juan Carlos Reyes held up the tuft of hair as a trophy. "Proof!"

Lilia spun away. "You're a fool. Fidel is not dead." She felt a comforting hand on her shoulder—the impersonator. A harmless fellow, she thought. And not a bad kisser.

Carefully, Reyes slipped the lock of hair into an inside pocket of his blazer. "Hector," he said. "Bring me the prize. Bring me the key to my destiny!"

"Cuba's destiny, you said."

"Whatever. Go get the damn thing."

Reyes himself cradled the Uzi while Hector retrieved the red cooler from the speedboat, which was tied to the yacht's stern. He brought the Gott into the salon and set it ceremoniously before Reyes's delicate loafers.

Lilia Sands and Mickey Schwartz had no idea what they were about to see. Excitedly, Juan Carlos shoved the machine gun butt-first at Hector, and flipped open the cooler. He removed a stainless canister the size of a hat-

box, and placed it—shiny and perspiring from the ice—
on a beveled glass dining table.

"Where was it?" Reyes asked breathlessly.

"Hidden in the woman's boat," Hector replied. "The
blonde's."

The stumpy millionaire chuckled. "Lost and then
found. Fate, no? That's what brought him to me. Fate in
the form of wild women." He stepped back from the canister. "Open it, Hector."

"*Sí.*"

"Let the bastard out!"

"OK, OK." Hector grappled with the canister's vacuum
lock until it surrendered with a burp. Cautiously, he
opened the lid.

"Take it out," Reyes commanded.

Hector hesitated. By nature he was not a squeamish
man, but . . .

"Take it out!"

Hector grabbed a gray mossy handful and lifted the
staring head from the canister. He held it like a lantern,
his arm outstretched toward the two captives. Mickey
Schwartz's mouth turned to chalk. Lilia lowered her eyes.

Juan Carlos Reyes was trembling with pleasure. "Señor
Castro, how nice of you to join us! You're looking very
jaunty this evening—wouldn't you agree, Miss Sands?"

Without comment Lilia collapsed into Mickey
Schwartz's arms. "Swell," he said with a grunt.

Reyes produced a gold-plated cuticle scissors and
snipped a thatch from the severed head. "Hector," he
said, "keep an eye on our guests. I'll be in the galley."

The DNA expert had been waiting three hours; a Harvard doctor, the best. "This is very exciting," Reyes said to himself, hurrying with the twin locks of hair out of the salon.

Hector kept the Uzi trained on his captives as he refit the Castro head in its container. Mickey Schwartz arranged the unconscious Lilia on a leather sofa. He pointed at the canister. "That's him, isn't it? The real deal."

"Shut up," said Hector, feeling creepy—Fidel's ugly face, everywhere he looked. He returned the canister to the red Gott cooler.

The bodyguard with the pearl in his nose appeared in the salon with Fay and Britt. Firmly, he placed them on tall stools at the bar. The women still looked queasy.

Mickey Schwartz said, "You missed quite a show."

Promptly, Hector whacked him with the back of his hand. "I told you to shut up."

Mickey shut up. He felt the yacht begin to rock under a freshening northern breeze. The slap of the waves grew louder against the hull.

Britt cynically motioned toward the red cooler. "How's the head?"

"What head?" said Hector with a wink. "Nothing but Snapples in there. Kiwi-flavored."

Fay looked up. "Randy, what's going to happen to us?"

Randy was the bodyguard with the nose stud. He furrowed his tan brow and blinked intently at Fay's question.

"Randy doesn't know what's going to happen to us," Britt Montero said wearily. "Randy barely knows how to dress himself."

Randy ambiguously clicked his teeth. Hector sighed.

"Sweetheart, there's *lots* of things Randy knows how to do, and he'll show you one in particular if you don't shut your fat trap."

Britt fell silent. Fay laid her head on the bar. Mickey Schwartz rubbed his jaw, and Lilia Sands stirred on the couch. Not a word was spoken for a long time, until Juan Carlos Reyes returned in an ebullient glow.

■　■　■

The human head for which Marion McAlister Williams had been paid close to a million dollars, and for which she had eventually been murdered, belonged not to Fidel Castro but to one of his Cuban doubles, a man named Rigoberto Lopez.

The purchaser of the head had been well aware it was not Castro's. The purchaser worked free-lance for the U.S. Central Intelligence Agency. His first name was Raymond; his last name was unknown, even to his own team.

Raymond and his people had been given to understand that a serious problem threatened the administration's top-secret plan to replace the Cuban dictator. The scheme—dreamed up at the NSC, presented in Havana by former president Carter, and ultimately endorsed by the ailing Castro himself—had been to trick Castro's enemies into believing he was dead by using a fake head. In exchange for leaving Cuba, Fidel had been promised a safe and secret exile, the best cancer specialists in the world, and a cash departure bonus equivalent to that paid to Baby Doc Duvalier, when he fled Haiti.

Raymond had been informed that the Castro plan was

in jeopardy, due to a surplus of bogus heads in Greater Miami. Raymond had also been told that the plan was so vital to national security that he was authorized to spend any sum of money to retrieve the extra heads before their existence became a public scandal.

Therefore Raymond had no qualms about giving a million in taxpayer funds to an eccentric old bird in Coconut Grove. The head in her refrigerator had been picked up in its steel canister and transported by a Coast Guard Citation jet to Washington, D.C., where it had been placed in a locked freezer in the basement of the State Department.

It was in no way Raymond's fault that the U.S. government had subsequently closed down because of a petty political squabble, or that a cost-conscious assistant undersecretary at the State Department had shut off electricity to the building's basement, or that the million-dollar head of Rigoberto Lopez was currently decomposing faster than your average wheel of cheap Brie.

Meanwhile Raymond was at the Alexander on Miami Beach, in a suite once occupied by Keith Richards. Raymond was a happy man. The sun was bright, the sky was blue, and he was interviewing a hack actor named Brandon Dash and a skittish makeup artist named Ziff Bodine. And Raymond had become totally convinced that the other surplus Castro head was only a clever movie prop, and that it was now safely suppurating in the belly of a lemon shark at a club named Hell.

Which left one remaining head—the important one, the correct one, the one with the notch in the ear. And that head, according to Raymond's contacts, was exactly where it was supposed to be.

Raymond made a brief, smug phone call to Washington. The man in Washington then made a call to Havana. The man in Havana then telephoned Miami Beach: the Odyssey Motel. Room 105.

Mike Weston grabbed it on the third ring. "What's the good news, *compadre?*"

A short pause, then: "Everything's fine. We found your lost luggage. Where is Hector?"

"On a seaplane flying home from Bimini."

"It went well?" asked the voice from Havana.

"Perfect. I expect him any minute," Weston said. "I'm already packing for Belize."

"Don't go anywhere until you hear from us. Don't leave the room—you understand?"

"Hey, you're the boss," Weston said.

"You do understand? Stay right where you are."

"I heard you the first time." Weston hung up the phone, stretched out on the starchy motel sheets, dialed up another porny film on Spectravision, and waited for Hector.

That's where Franklin and Marlis found them later, their insides decorating the room.

■　　■　　■

Aboard the *Entrante Presidente,* the captives were served lobster fritters and a tangy mango sorbet. Hunger overcame their pride and anxiety.

Juan Carlos Reyes, who was in a celebratory mood, told them what would come next. "Of course you will not be killed, because there's no need. A small launch will take you from my yacht to the Big Game Club in Bimini. There you'll be met by Bahamian customs and immigration officers. For the next several days, you will have a most difficult time trying to return to Miami."

Britt Montero started to speak, but the millionaire cut her off. "Miss Montero, don't ever think about calling in a story to your newspaper. Your cellular has already been disabled and your accommodations in Bimini, unfortunately, will be too rustic for telephone jacks."

Britt said, "You'll never get away with it."

"Oh, I will. Easily, in fact. By the time you get out, I'll be on my way to Havana."

Angrily, Fay Leonard said, "You can't silence us."

"Nor would I want to," said Juan Carlos Reyes. "Miss Leonard, I'll have my own version of these events, which will be substantiated by an esteemed scientist from Harvard, and also by Mr. Schwartz, if he still wishes to be paid for his services."

Mickey hung his head.

"My recollection," Reyes went on, "is that Miss Leonard and Miss Montero, having heard of my million-dollar offer for proof of Castro's death, greedily attempted to defraud me. They constructed a flimsy hoax involving a Castro impersonator and a delusional old woman, Miss Sands, in the hopes I'd fall for it—"

"That's ridiculous!" Fay shouted.

"Maybe, maybe not." Reyes took a sip of rum. "Miss Montero, do your readers know how little your newspaper pays you? A million dollars would buy lots of cat food, no?"

Britt chewed her lower lip, and thought of her callow young editors. Assuming her story would eventually get published, she wondered what she could possibly write about the severed heads that would make any sense.

Juan Carlos Reyes rose. "Randy will take you to the launch." He bowed slightly toward Lilia. "I'm sorry your heart is broken, Miss Sands, but I'm not at all sorry your infamous lover is dead. My only regret is that I didn't kill him myself."

"As if you could," Lilia said venomously. "Little cockroach that you are. Cowardly limp-noodled—"

"Enough," Mickey Schwartz cut in.

"—rotten little crook!"

Juan Carlos Reyes wagged a mocking finger at Lilia Sands. "Now is that any way," he asked, "to address the next president of a free Cuba?"

■　　■　　■

It was a good plan; a solid plan. A plan that would've worked, if only the real Fidel Castro had not been insulted, propositioned, and mugged in broad daylight on Miami Beach.

The messy murders of the two men in room 105—that hadn't bothered Castro, for he'd known of it in advance. He even knew what the police still did not know: the victims' names (Hector Pupo and Mike Weston), and why they'd had to die (they were loud, careless, and knew too much).

A security matter handled by experts who made it look amateurish—Fidel understood such things.

However, the arrival of the perky cleanup crew had put him on edge. Castro was rattled by the knowledge that murders were so common in South Florida that swabbing up crime scenes was a full-time trade, and evidently a lucrative one.

Franklin and Marlis, the workers who came to room 105, were too talky and inquisitive. They stared dubiously at Fidel's Korean-made toupee, and posed snoopy questions disguised as banter. Fidel, as usual, pretended not to understand English. It was all he could do not to retch during Franklin's graphic monologue about the effects of gastric acids on suede upholstery.

Castro realized that if Franklin and Marlis somehow recognized him, they could with one well-placed phone call generate more business for themselves, and perhaps even the gratuity of a lifetime. Once Castro gave a subtle tug on his good earlobe, three stocky men in guayaberas materialized to escort the voluble cleaners off the premises. Meanwhile Fidel slipped into his room and changed into a bathing suit, an absurd vermilion slingshot which was (Cuban intelligence had assured him) the prevailing beachside attire of old, pallid, pudgy male tourists.

The outfit worked too well, the swimsuit a beacon. Strolling alone on the sand, Fidel was scarcely a hundred yards from the motel when a gum-popping prostitute offered to "rock your world, Gramps," for fifty U.S. dollars. Her efforts at detaching his red thong were interrupted by a wiry ferret-eyed man who roughly knocked Castro

down, stuck a pistol in his belly, and stripped off the gold
Cartier wristwatch he'd received as a gift on a state visit to
Paris.

Fidel didn't recognize the robber, but he recognized
the prison tattoos on the man's grimy knuckles. Com-
binado del Este! With amazement Castro realized he was
being mugged by a thug that he himself had sprung from
prison and put on a boat to Key West in 1980. The bleak
beautiful irony made him cough up blood.

Numbed by the morphine, Fidel felt more indignity
than pain as the mugger ran away. Before the old man
could rise to his knees, a red-haired urchin no older than
six plucked the hairpiece from his scalp and dashed down
the beach, shouting to his mother that he'd found a dead
crow.

Castro, feeling himself hoisted by the armpits, reason-
ably anticipated dismemberment or evisceration.

"Easy," said the voice, which belonged to a motel security guard. The cheap badge on his shirt said "Joe Sereno." Fidel was grateful to see him.

"You all right?" Sereno asked. "Man, you don't look so
good."

In perfect English, Castro gasped, "What is this crazi-
ness? These monsters?"

"Just another day at the beach." Sereno smiled rue-
fully. "The problem, see, it started when they went to
topless. The guys, old tourist guys like yourself, come
down here to stare at the cuties. Am I right? The gangs,
hookers, scumbags—they all know this. So they hang on
this stretch, just waiting."

Fidel morosely dusted the grit from his chest. Sereno gently led him back toward the Odyssey. "I mean, you're a criminal it's not such a bad deal. Get a tan. Enjoy the naked babes. Mug a few Germans and Canadians, and that's your day."

"Why," rasped Castro, "aren't these terrible people in jail!"

Joe Sereno burst out laughing. "Where you from, old-timer—Mars? Come on, let me take you back to your room."

"Thank you, officer."

"By the way, there's something I gotta ask."

Fidel's jaws clenched. The security guy was eyeing him closer now, the way the cleaners had.

"Your name," said Sereno, "it's not really Garcia, is it?"

■　　■　　■

Less than two hours later, a chartered Gulfstream jet landed at the Opa-Locka airport, where it was met by a black Chevy Blazer. Four men got out and moved toward the plane. The tallest one walked slowly, as if in pain. The others could be seen helping him up the stairs. Minutes later, a station wagon arrived and a fifth person, a woman in a long gown, was led to the jet.

The flight plan indicated the Gulfstream would be heading nonstop to Kingston, Jamaica. This was a fib. The destination was Havana. Fidel Castro was going home to die.

Miami was too damn scary. The deal was off.

■ ■ ■

The remaining severed head, the one Juan Carlos Reyes imagined would make him president of Cuba, belonged to another expendable Castro double, José Paz-Gutierrez. This fact was known to Castro himself, Cuban State Security, the CIA, and of course Lilia Sands, who—on numerous long-ago lonely nights, when Fidel was away—had slept with José Paz-Gutierrez at a farmhouse in Camagüey. Of course she'd saved a lock of José's hair, as she did for all her lovers.

No one was less surprised than Lilia when Reyes's DNA expert matched with .9999995 certainty the hair from Lilia's cigar box with the severed head in the red Gott cooler. Her secret glee at fooling the munchkin-sized millionaire was tempered by a pang of wistfulness, for of all the Castro doubles Lilia had slept with, José Paz-Gutierrez had been the best—the one whose embrace most reminded her of Fidelito himself, the one whose earlobe she had once chomped off in ecstasy, just as she had Fidel's.

In fact, though Lilia wouldn't dare confess it, José Paz-Gutierrez definitely had Castro beat in one department, lovemaking-wise. The ardent José had a much longer . . . attention span, if you will. Lilia wondered if that's what had gotten him killed, as Castro's jealous streak was well known.

So she had mixed feelings on this special Friday morning. Oh, she was glad to be back in Havana, holding Fidel's hand as a fussy *gringo* tried to restore the illusion of vitality—gluing on the frizzy beard, aligning a new toupee, ruddying the cheeks, powdering the shadows around the hollowing eyes.

Still, Lilia took no joy in knowing that across the Florida Straits, the head of poor José Paz-Gutierrez soon would be boorishly displayed for all to see, like a taxidermied fish. Oh well, Lilia thought, it's all for the cause.

As she stroked Fidel's arm, hairless from chemotherapy, she observed a pale stripe on his wrist.

"Where is your watch?" she asked.

"Miami," Castro said sullenly.

"What happened?"

"I got mugged," he said, grimacing at the memory, "by a Marielito. Go ahead and laugh."

"I'm not laughing." Lilia turned, covered her mouth. "Honestly, Fidel, I'm *not.*"

■　　■　　■

The massive televised rally arranged at Miami's Torch of Friendship by Juan Carlos Reyes was not seen by:

• Britt Montero and Fay Leonard, who were sharing bare cinder-block quarters at the South Bimini airfield, under the supervision of an armed Bahamas customs officer;

• Mickey Schwartz, who was gambling away his ten-thousand-dollar payday on Paradise Island, where none of the cute croupiers seemed remotely amused by his stand-up impression of Howard Stern;

• Jake Lassiter, who was in a Flagler Street hot tub with the lukewarm ex-wife of his ex-client John Deal;

• John Deal, who was on Bird Road shopping for a red Testarossa to go with his black Bentley convertible;

• Marlis and Franklin, who were literally mopping up after a fatal cocaine dispute at a FEMA trailer court in Homestead;

• Joe Sereno, who was thanking a police review board for reinstating him, and promising to be more careful when arresting incontinent tourists;

• and Jimmy Carter, who was in Havana for a rare public appearance and historic announcement by Fidel Castro.

So absorbed in the pomp of his "preinauguration" was Juan Carlos Reyes that he remained unaware of events unfolding simultaneously in Cuba, unaware he was about to share a TV screen five stories high with the same man whose severed noggin he intended to unveil, unaware that local television stations were already receiving a live satellite feed from the presidential palace in Havana.

So that at the climactic moment when Juan Carlos Reyes victoriously hoisted a bearded head for all America to see, a very similar but undead head emerged on a sun-bleached balcony in Cuba. There the real Castro announced a liberal new human rights policy that freed every political prisoner, including (not coincidentally) two of Lilia Sands's nephews.

In Miami, the cheers at the Torch of Friendship ebbed into a confused mass murmuring as the crowd struggled to understand what they were seeing on the huge split screen. On one side was Reyes, waving the goggle-eyed head and proclaiming himself the harbinger of a new democracy in Cuba. On the other side, flanked by former president Carter, was a person who looked very much like Castro, and very much like he was still breathing.

Juan Carlos Reyes sensed the audience was no longer enthralled by his oratory. He spun around and saw what they saw on the giant TV screen.

"Noooooo!" The millionaire wheeled, bellowing into the thicket of microphones. "It's a trick! Can't you see, here is Castro!" He shook the head like a tambourine. "I can prove it, I can prove this is Fidel's head!"

Reyes was handicapped by the fact that, despite his wealth and power, he was not very popular in the exile community. For many years, Cuban-Americans had endured his grandiose promises, vituperative politics, and heavy-handed fund-raising tactics. Now this: a phony Castro head! It was too much.

Members of the crowd registered their scorn by hurling rocks, bottles, and ripe coconuts at Juan Carlos Reyes, who fled the stage at a dead run. He showed fair speed for a short-legged fellow, but the mob chasing him through Bayfront Park was fueled by outrage. When Reyes reached the seawall, he hesitated only briefly before diving into Biscayne Bay. The bearded head went with him.

■   ■   ■

While Booger didn't know much, he did know where human idiots liked to run their speedboats. From traumatic experience he'd learned to remain submerged in the busiest lanes of the bay, especially the waters between Dodge Island and Bayfront Park.

Thus Booger and his new female friend, having taken a

prodigious breath, were safely coasting across the bottom when the yellow Donzi full of would-be playboys roared out of Bayside Marketplace. The boat swung south at the ridiculous speed of fifty-eight knots. At its helm was a seventeen-year-old trust fund troglodyte, culturally intoxicated by his first visit to Hooter's.

Reflexively, Booger glanced upward at the approaching growl of the Donzi. Fifteen feet above him, haplessly flailing into the boat's path, was a man in a business suit. One of his hands clutched something round and mossy-looking, though it definitely wasn't a head of lettuce.

The Booger of forty-eight hours before—the febrile, erratic Booger with Flipperian fantasies—might have been reminded of poor old Marion, might have shot upward to rescue this wallowing specimen from the deadly propellers that had claimed so many of Booger's dearest manatee companions.

But the new Booger knew better. The notion of playing hero never entered his unconvoluted brain, which at the moment was singularly focused on procreation. Thirteen hundred pounds of saucy sea cow nooky had paddled into Booger's life, and he was serene beyond distraction.

So he dismissed the human commotion on the surface of the bay; lowered his shoe button eyes and swam onward, nudging and nuzzling his slippery new mate. Booger might have flinched slightly at the familiar thud of the impact above, the sickening whine of cavitating props, but he didn't look up a second time.

Every mammal for himself.